I0578035

C.W. Allen

The Secret Benefits of Invisibility

Published by: Cinnabar Moth Publishing LLC
Santa Fe, New Mexico

Cover Design by: Ira Geneve

ISBN-13: 978-1-953971-47-0
Library of Congress Control Number: 2022936851

The Secret Benefits of Invisibility

C.W. ALLEN

CHAPTER 1
READING, WRITING, AND RUMORS

Snowflakes the size of baseballs were falling outside, which was ironic, since baseball didn't exist anymore.

Zed had never cared much for organized sports, so the loss of baseball wasn't so horrible, in his opinion. He cared a great deal about snow, however. In his last house, he'd had a favorite windowsill in the upstairs hallway that was deep enough to sit in and read while looking out the window. Cloudy fall afternoons made for excellent reading weather, but an early morning snowfall was even better, because school might get canceled, and then he'd get to stay home and read as long as he liked. That was before the move, though. His new home had school too, of course, but no windowsills. You don't need windowsills in a place with no windows.

His older sister Tuesday was not such a fan of the

"organized" aspect of baseball—she'd had some unusual barriers to making friends in her last town, not least among them her name, and it's tough to play baseball by yourself—but she did enjoy sports, because sports are something you can win. You can't *win* at reading a book in a windowsill. And anyway, she reminded Zed, baseball technically still existed, somewhere. It's just that no one else in Falinnheim had ever heard of it.

"I wish we could go out and play in it," Tuesday grumbled, glaring at the thick fluffy flakes taunting her through the security monitor. "Even *you* liked building snow forts."

"I liked the building part," Zed agreed. "But then you insisted on throwing snowballs at me the moment we finished building it. And you *always* won at snowball fights."

"Darn right, I did," Tuesday muttered.

"You *know* why we can't go outside," said their father.

They knew, all right. Two months ago, when they'd been transported to this hidden pocket of the Earth's geography, they'd spent the whole first week being kidnapped alternately by soldiers, bandits, and the secret police of Falinnheim's murderous dictator, Tyrren. The bandits turned out to be resistance fighters, which was why the entire Furst family had decided to take refuge in their secret base. The soldiers, known as the Legion, and the secret police, the Red Hand, would love nothing more than to get their hands on the children of Falinnheim's last surviving royalty. Which was why Zed and Tuesday had not set foot outside the refurbished mine the Resistance called home in over two months.

Months didn't exist anymore either, Tuesday remembered with a sigh.

As much as Zed and Tuesday hated being stuck inside missing a perfectly good snow day, it was nothing compared to the sullen resentment painted across their father's features. He propped his bandaged leg up on the control panel of the surveillance office, nearly upsetting the steaming mug his partner had balanced there, and glared icy daggers at the beautiful scene. "No place like home, huh?" he muttered to no one in particular.

"I'm sure Doctor Ubime will have you fixed up in no time," Zed offered, with questionable conviction. Zed had every faith in the doctor's skill, but he had to admit the pace of progress was disheartening. After weeks of treatment for a smashed foot, his father had graduated from crutches to a soft protective boot, but he still was still limping.

His father grunted in reply.

A twang of guilt pricked the pit of Tuesday's stomach. Her father had been injured protecting them from soldiers intent on turning them over to Tyrren. Which was heroic, she wanted to argue! But the plan that got them captured in the first place had been her idea, and the tiny voice at the back of her mind insisted on bringing it up with irritating regularity. She shook the thought loose. No, it wasn't her fault… after all, Dad couldn't go out on missions with the other Resistance agents anyway, not with half the soldiers in Falinnheim looking for him.

Zed and Tuesday finished the last bites of their breakfast, said goodbye to their father and the other security officer on duty, and wandered out of the surveillance office to gather their things for school.

<hr>

In many ways, the base's school was much the same as others Tuesday and Zed had attended, back when things like baseball and months and windows still made sense. There were lots of other kids living in the high-tech converted mine—children of the rebel fighters, and refugees squeezed out of society by Tyrren's oppressive grip. And orphans, of course. Murderous dictators tend to leave behind a lot of orphans. They were all expected to rotate through the base's various duty stations, pitching in where they could to help run this underground village, and getting a taste of the professions they might choose for apprenticeships when they were old enough. But that still left lots of down time, and without baseball games to play and snow forts to build, that time was spent on school.

There was one class for the youngest children—the ones still learning reading and spelling and counting—and another for the older kids who could already spell and count and read, but needed something to keep them busy until they were old enough to choose an apprenticeship. Their teacher, Professor Orpin, liked to say this class was devoted to "higher-level reasoning." But in Tuesday's experience, a lot of school time was devoted to other endeavors. Like passing notes. Doodling in the margins of their notebooks. And, of course, thinking up embarrassing nicknames for each other.

Tuesday was prepared for this part. In her last school, her unusual name had been like bully catnip. She could tell instantly when meeting someone whether they were going to be a problem. The mean ones always zoned out with an eager gleam in their eyes the instant they heard her name, because they had stopped participating in the forced social interaction and were now setting all their brain cells on the task of thinking up calendar puns to lob at her later, when there were no adults around to critique their work.

Back on her first day at the base's school, as she and Zed had slouched at the front of the class being introduced, a realization struck—Falinnheim didn't use last names! Sure, she couldn't dodge the "Tuesday" part, but maybe if no one tacked on the "June" and "Furst," she'd be able to slide by unscathed.

Even in a parallel dimension, or however Falinnheim's "Earth, but not" location could be described, it seemed teachers were fond of putting people on the spot. Professor Orpin clapped twice for everyone's attention and then prodded Tuesday and Zed forward. "Another family has joined us," he called. "Please welcome our new students."

All around the room, kids looked up from their work.

There were no desks, or even chairs; some kids burrowed into sack cushions or sprawled on sofas, knelt on the floor constructing model robots or stood at work benches. One boy even paced the room with his nose buried in a book, walking laps as he read.

This is it, Tuesday reminded herself. *A fresh start. Clean slate. New home, new school, new life. I can be whoever I want.* She tried to conjure up something clever (or at least not embarrassing) to say, but found her brain shackled by that special brand of amnesia that comes from trying to squash your entire personality into a witty quip. Specks of dust lit by the crystal bulbs overhead wafted in slow motion, as though floating through syrup instead of air. Her thoughts felt syrupy too.

The teacher cleared his throat and gave Tuesday a significant look. Oh well—stalling didn't usually work, but it had been worth a shot.

"Hi." Tuesday offered a feeble wave. "I'm Tuesday, and this is my brother Zed."

Silence. Not a single giggle. Not even suppressed snorting! So far, so good…

At the back of the room, an older girl with her hair in long golden ringlets raised her hand, but then spit out her comment without waiting to be called on. "Where are you from?"

"Uhhh…" Tuesday turned to Zed. They held a silent conversation with their eyebrows—the General had made clear that the existence of other worlds beyond Falinnheim was strictly classified information. But they had to say *something*…

"New Angkor," Zed supplied.

It would have to do, Tuesday decided. That was the first village they'd visited, when the smuggler who'd interrupted two of Falinnheim's soldiers trying to kidnap them had used his contraband compass to bring them over from the "other" Earth. She realized she actually had no idea where her parents had lived before leaving Falinnheim sixteen years ago.

"You're the ones with the Gabriel Hound," said the kid who was still pacing and reading. It wasn't a question, and he didn't look up as he said it. In fact, all Tuesday could see of his face was a strip of warm brown forehead topped with bouncy blue-black curls, because the rest of it was still hidden behind the cover of *Cryptozoology and You: Real, Extinct, or Imaginary?*

"That's my mom's pet," Zed answered the not-a-question.

"Nuh-uh," said the book kid. "We can't have pets inside the base. And regular pets don't make adults nervous. People turn around if they see that hound heading down the halls. They're afraid. They lie about it if you say so, though."

"That's enough, Fariq," said Professor Orpin. He walked to his desk and pulled an electronic tablet out of the top drawer. He smiled a little too brightly over at his new students, trying to change the subject. "Let's add your birthdays to our class list, shall we?"

Changing the subject was just fine with Tuesday. "I'll be thirteen on March eleventh," she volunteered.

Now there was laughter. What was so funny about that? Tuesday couldn't think of anything controversial about a birthday, no matter when it was. Even kids born on leap day or Halloween usually treated it as a badge of honor, not something to keep under wraps.

"The first ten marches weren't enough?" a redheaded girl near the front whispered to her friend, who promptly dissolved into giggles.

Tuesday shot a confused look at her brother, who offered half a shrug in return.

"I'm ten," Zed added. "But almost eleven. My birthday is next month, actually—October twenty-first."

More laughter. Professor Orpin looked up from his notes. "Be serious, please. I know it's tempting to make jokes when you're new and trying to fit in, but I do actually need to know your birthdates."

A tiny, freckle-faced boy kneeling on the rug raised his hand. He couldn't have been older than about eight, Tuesday guessed—probably the youngest one in the class.

The teacher sighed, but as the giggling hadn't died down yet he decided to indulge the question. "Yes, Linus?"

The boy's pale features rearranged themselves into a mask of confusion. "What's an... October?"

Zed pulled out his notebook and began scribbling.

————————

If the first day of school had been a disappointment, the next few weeks hadn't done much to improve things. Gossip started swirling almost immediately. Of course there was no way to keep Nyx a secret—any massive black dog would tend to draw the eye, but a massive black dog that most of Falinnheim grew up hearing terrifying legends about sent the rumor mill into high gear. Taking her for a walk to the garden wing was like strolling around with a velociraptor on a leash. Not that Nyx would stoop to actually wearing a leash, of course, but that's how everyone reacted. Book Kid was right; some people stared, mouths dangling open like gasping fish. Others skidded to a halt when they saw her coming and "suddenly remembered" they were heading the wrong direction. Anyone willing to wander casually through the halls in Nyx's company earned the same suspicion—namely, Tuesday and Zed.

Then there was their mother. She tried to keep a casual profile and smiled warmly at everyone she passed in the halls, but there was no hiding the fact that she happened to look exactly like the princess who'd gone missing from Alexandria sixteen years ago, presumed murdered by Tyrren's lackeys. Because that happened to be exactly who she was. It didn't matter if she went by her real name, Theadora (she did not tack on the Princess part, Zed noticed) or stuck with the "Zora Furst" alias Tuesday and Zed grew up knowing people were going to point and whisper.

Their father was not a celebrity. He had started to go by his Falinnheim name again, but it didn't matter. Arden Furst, or Beren the Vigilant—no one at the base seemed to know or care that he'd once been a palace guard. They were far more interested to learn that their leader, their General, the legendary Green Fly in Tyrren's ointment, had a son. It was a good thing her right-hand man Captain Solomon wasn't the jealous type, because the base was buzzing with the notion that a rift had formed in the chain of command.

The General, naturally, refused to dignify such nonsense with any sort of comment. Which seemed to be a thing with her, since she didn't comment on much of anything, ever. Even to her newly discovered grandchildren.

Now that the cat was out of the bag about Falinnheim's existence, and their family's place in its history, Tuesday and Zed had hoped that all the secrets would be out in the open. But their parents' new jobs with the Resistance leadership and security teams were just as secretive as ever. The kids would often arrive back at the family's living quarters after school to find their parents discussing something in heated whispers, then fall silent when they entered the room. And when Tuesday and Zed fended off Nyx's slobbery greeting and asked what was going on, the answer was always the same: "Sorry, we can't talk about it. Classified."

Not-so-subtle whispers had become the soundtrack to Zed and Tuesday's lives.

The not-even-remotely subtle problems were yet to come.

EXCERPT FROM ZED'S NOTEBOOK ABOUT FALINNHEIM'S CALENDAR

Back on the first day of school I asked Mom and Dad why our birthdays had everyone confused. They explained Falinnheim uses a different calendar system than we're used to. *(They could have thought to mention this earlier!)*

- No months, only seasons.
- But there are FIVE seasons for some reason? 73 days each
- Kinda makes sense though. 365 days in a year doesn't divide equally by four, but $365 \div 5 = 73$
- Seasons are:

  Endeavor *(spring, planting crops)*

  Diligence *(early summer, growing the stuff you planted)*

  Bounty *(late summer and early fall, harvest)*

  Providence *(late fall and early winter, food preservation and holidays)*

  Reflection *(late winter, getting ready for the next planting season)*

- This must be traditional or something, because the base grows stuff all year round in the greenhouse wing.

- No months, but I think they must still use weeks? No one asked what a "Tuesday" was.

CONCLUSION:

Need more data. Maybe ask Grandma? If she's ever not busy when I see her. *(Which so far is never…)*

Also, need to warm her up to the idea of being called "Grandma." So far—she doesn't seem thrilled. But *no way* am I spending the rest of my life calling her "the General."

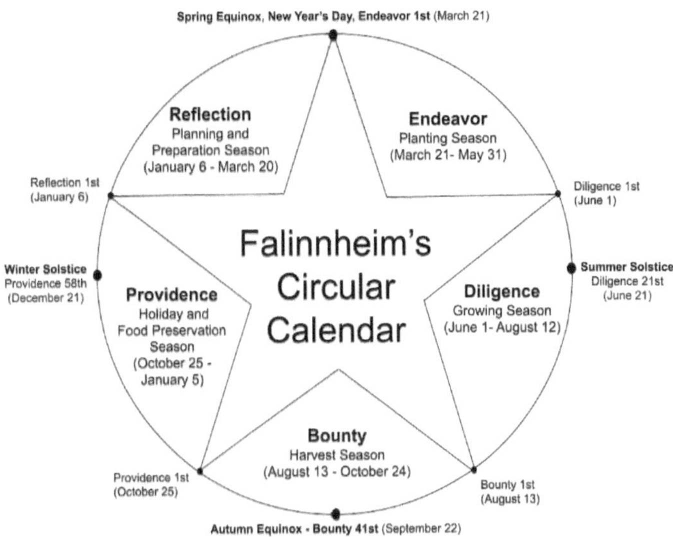

Spring Equinox, New Year's Day, Endeavor 1st (March 21)
Reflection
Planning and Preparation Season
(January 6 - March 20)
Endeavor
Planting Season
(March 21- May 31)
Reflection 1st
(January 6)
Diligence 1st
(June 1)
Winter Solstice
Providence 58th
(December 21)
Falinnheim's Circular Calendar
Summer Solstice
Diligence 21st
(June 21)
Providence
Holiday and Food Preservation Season
(October 25 - January 5)
Diligence
Growing Season
(June 1- August 12)
Bounty
Harvest Season
(August 13 - October 24)
Providence 1st
(October 25)
Bounty 1st
(August 13)
Autumn Equinox - Bounty 41st (September 22)

CHAPTER 2
BIRDS OF A
FEATHER

Zed was used to feeling slightly out of step with his peers, as though he were the one guarding unusual secrets, instead of his parents. But three months into this pilgrimage to his family's homeland, he was still plagued by moments that went way beyond a slight misalignment. It felt more like climbing stairs in the dark and believing there's one more step at the top than there really is. Every time he discovered some new detail about life in Falinnheim that everyone else took for granted, his stomach jolted like his foot was falling through empty air on that nonexistent top step, the framework he'd trusted in suddenly missing.

First, there was the whole calendar thing. Luckily the teacher had frowned down a couple students' suggestions that anyone who didn't have a grasp on five basic seasons might really belong in the younger class. But Zed couldn't shake the notion that he'd been labeled *stupid* right then and there, and would spend the rest of his life wearing it like an imaginary nametag on his shirt. With the new calendar came unfamiliar holidays: the autumn equinox celebration was pretty self-explanatory, but Halloween had been replaced with Samhain, with more focus on changing seasons and departed ancestors than goblins, ghouls, and gaudy mounds of candy. But the thing that really took the biscuit was the dodos.

He'd heard them mentioned in his first week at the Resistance base, even before his parents joined the underground (literally) party (not literally—in fact even routine tasks were treated as deadly serious.) But it was well into December (oops; *"Providence"*) before he and Tuesday had their first duty assignment in the poultry wing. This was the earliest shift they'd ever been assigned, before the dining hall would even open for breakfast, so their father offered them some jerky from the security team's emergency rations in case they got hungry in the meantime. Zed triple-checked the pockets of his school uniform tunic before leaving his family's quarters to get to work. He was *not* about to get his first glimpse of a supposedly extinct creature in the flesh without a notebook and pencil handy for a few sketches.

Even Tuesday had to admit she was intrigued. Usually she made a point of brushing off Falinnheim's eccentricities, partly because she didn't want to seem impressed by a place she'd had no choice about moving to, and partly because she wasn't ready to admit her living situation was anything more than a temporary inconvenience. But she couldn't turn down a front-row seat to something no one back home would ever get to see. Not that she could tell anyone about it when she got back, of course—no one would believe her anyway. But she liked the idea of tucking the experience away to savor privately. It made her feel... *important.* Boring people don't have mysterious secrets.

They had to ask directions in the halls since they were still learning their way around the sprawling maze of underground corridors, but managed to arrive at the gate to the poultry wing more or less on time. A dozen other people were already waiting for the shift supervisor to check them in and unlock the doors—adults, mostly, though they did recognize two other kids from Professor Orpin's class. Celia, a tall and lanky fourteen-year-old, bounced her fingers absently through her straw-blonde curls as if she feared they might deflate if she didn't keep them properly aerated. She waited next to a man who could only be her father—same long, reedy arms and square nose, but his yellow curls were cropped too short to tell if they required fluffing for proper maintenance. Fariq was crouched in a corner, trying to squeeze in a few last sentences of *The Children's Psychology Primer* before the supervisor made him stow his book away and begin work. At least, Zed was pretty sure that was his name. He was embarrassed to realize that three months into sharing a classroom, he still thought of the quiet eleven-year-old as Book Kid. He thought about going over to say hi, but spent so long debating whether maybe Fariq would rather not be bothered while reading that his turn in the check-in line arrived, and the opportunity slipped by.

"Right," the supervisor announced when she'd unlocked the doors. "If this is your first shift in the poultry wing, please partner with someone who's worked here before and can show you the ropes."

Zed looked around. The poultry wing was a spacious open room, something like a roller-skating rink, but with a dirt floor in place of polished planks, and bright overhead lighting instead of a disco ball. The dull droning of hidden ventilation fans muddied his concentration. It was like trying to focus while taking a test, only to have his thoughts ambushed by that annoying humming sound fluorescent lightbulbs make when everything is too quiet. If there was anything he missed about the "other Earth," fluorescent lights definitely didn't make the list.

He turned to Tuesday, who was looking around for familiar faces. Her doubtful frown showed they were thinking the same thing—latching on to a total stranger wasn't an appealing idea. Maybe Celia could fill them in? They had never really talked to her in class; as the oldest of Professor Orpin's students, she usually worked alone on subjects the others weren't ready for. And besides, she and her father were already emerging from the supply room with rakes. The only person not already working with a partner was—

"Hi."

Tuesday jumped. She hadn't noticed Fariq standing next to her until he spoke. He stared across the open arena, nearly deserted now as everyone else was gathering their equipment. He didn't look at Zed and Tuesday as he continued. "We should let the birds out. They're done sleeping."

"You've worked here before?" Zed asked.

"Yeah," he said, and slouched toward a set of wide wooden doors near the equipment office. "Come on."

Tuesday frowned at Zed. He shrugged back and followed Fariq. At least now they had a guide.

Fariq lifted the latch and stepped back to let the doors swing slowly open. An avalanche of dodos poured out, brushing past them like a flock of short, grumpy businessmen in dusty gray suits, impatiently bustling around a train station on their way somewhere more important.

Zed jumped out of the way and whipped out his notebook and pencil. Tuesday jumped too, but more in alarm than amazement.

"Augh!" she yelled. "Why are they so *big*?" She flinched away as one of the dodos brushed past her leg. Its bald, leathery face came all the way up to her hip.

Zed was too busy sketching to look up. "What were you expecting?"

"I don't know!" Tuesday blathered. "Smaller, I guess! Slower. Dumber. More like chickens!"

It would have taken a Leaning Tower of Chickens stacked three high to see eye to eye with a dodo. They looked like gigantic turkeys with their tail feathers plucked and stunted wings tucked in by their sides, with bulbous bike horns for heads. It was like someone cobbled together a Frankenbird out of spare parts as a prank.

"It's okay," said Fariq in his customary monotone. "Bird phobias are really common. I don't like spiders much, myself."

"I'm not *afraid* of them," Tuesday protested. "Just… surprised."

Celia brushed past them with her rake, dropping a derisive chuckle as she passed. "Honestly, it's like you've never seen a common dodo before. You panic about worms in the garden wing too? Or is Her Highness too important to get her hands dirty with the commoners?"

Tuesday scowled. "What's *that* supposed to mean?"

Celia whirled around to face her. "Nobody asked your family to swoop in and take over, you know. And just because your mom has some fancy title and a spooky pet and you're related to the General doesn't mean you get special treatment."

"I never asked for any!" Tuesday shot back. "And the Gen—I mean Grandm—whoever… she works just like everyone else. And so do my parents!"

"Whatever," said Celia as she continued toward the coop. "Your mom's probably making it up anyway."

Tuesday aimed a glare at her back, but said nothing.

The chickens emerged next, heads bobbing cautiously as they peered around to see if the advance wave of dodos had been massacred by anything worth squawking the alarm about. When no ambush emerged, they set to work pecking and scratching at the dirt floor.

A dodo circled back through the crowd and paused at Tuesday's knee.

Tuesday sucked in a breath and froze. The dodo craned its neck to squint accusingly up at her with one beady eye. After a long, silent inspection, it leaned down and clamped its beak onto her shin.

Tuesday was tempted to punt the arrogant thing like a football, but settled for dodging backward with a yelp.

"They bite," said Fariq.

"I noticed!" Tuesday yelled back, massaging her leg.

Zed feverishly scribbled more notes underneath his dodo sketch.

"Half of you on coop duty," the supervisor called over the chaos. "The other half grab shields and line the parade route."

"*Parade?*" Tuesday spit at Fariq. "What is this, some sadistic new holiday? Monster Turkey Appreciation Day?"

Zed didn't know what was going on either, but after Tuesday's introduction to the birds, shields were starting to sound like a wise precaution.

Fariq didn't answer. He plodded over to the equipment office and emerged with three rectangular metal panels, each about the size of a pizza box. He handed two of them over to Zed and Tuesday.

"We have to herd them to the garden wing," he explained. "We block the halls we don't want them to go down with these."

"Why the garden wing? Zed asked.

"So they can garden," said Fariq blankly, as though this should have been obvious.

Zed shrugged and accepted the shield. Tuesday glowered, but took hers too. "*That* should be a riot. Do we have to dress them up with tiny rakes and sun hats first?"

One by one, workers slipped out the door while the supervisor shooed the impatient birds back. Tuesday and Zed stationed themselves an arm's length apart, halfway down the hall that connected the poultry wing to the greenhouse. Across from them, Fariq modeled how to hold their shields in front of their legs without completely crouching down, which would have put their faces at pecking height. The last person in line double-checked that the greenhouse was empty, then mashed a big red override button to keep the automatic double doors ajar.

"Ready?" the supervisor called.

Everyone nodded grimly. Tuesday gripped her shield tighter and leaned as far back as she could without dropping it. And then the supervisor opened up the floodgates.

It was less like a parade, and more like the Running of The Bulls. The dodos led the charge, their scaly yellow feet pattering along the polished floor with surprising speed. The chickens followed, less timid now, jostling each other for a place in the stampede. When the last bird passed, the first two people in line dropped out of formation and guarded the poultry wing doors so no one could change their minds and turn around. They walked slowly forward, using their shields to usher the stragglers down the hall. When the last bird crossed the threshold into the greenhouse, all the workers laid their shields on the floor and followed them in.

"That was *amazing*!" Tuesday gushed as she abandoned her shield and found a place in the crowd. "Let's do that again!" (Apparently a little adrenaline was enough to help her over her hesitancy, Zed theorized with a grin.)

"Oh, we will," said Fariq. "In about twenty minutes. We'll have to herd them back to the poultry wing. And they're not as excited about going back."

Zed pulled his notebook out again and looked around the greenhouse. The birds had made themselves at home, hopping into the raised beds in search of insects and sprouting weeds, the larger dodos patrolling the aisles for any bruised or overripe fruit that had been left behind during the previous day's harvest. He took a seat on the ledge of a planting bed and finished jotting down his observations. Now he understood why Fariq had called this excursion "gardening"—the birds were making short work of cleaning up all the little details that would require too much crouching over and searching under leaves for humans to do. And though animals with beaks couldn't *smile,* exactly, they definitely seemed to be enjoying the task.

As it always did when he focused on taking notes, time slipped away from Zed like a greased otter. It seemed like he'd barely sat down when the supervisor appeared and announced it was time to do the whole operation again in reverse.

He and Tuesday took their places in the hall and hoisted their shields into place. By this time the workers who'd stayed behind to collect eggs and rake out the coop had grabbed more shields and joined the line, so everyone stood shoulder to shoulder instead of spaced out.

It took six ushers to sweep the birds out of various greenhouse nooks and into the hall. There was a lot of clucking and indignant flapping going on. Apparently heading back to the coop was a less appealing prospect than a treasure hunt for fruit and bugs. And like toddlers resisting bedtime, they were using every trick in the book to delay the process: hiding in the taller plants, running circles around the workers, and one of the bolder dodos even stalked toward an usher's shield, daring him to keep insisting snack time was over.

Finally they got the last stragglers rounded up. The return procession was slower than the trip there, but the birds went along without too much fuss. Tuesday was even beginning to relax a bit and hold her shield without leaning so far back. She let out an anxious breath as the last dodo passed her. "See?" she said to no one in particular. "Nothing to it."

Zed was debating whether to congratulate her bravery, or whether that might disrupt her illusion of never having been nervous in the first place, when his thoughts were interrupted by some commotion further up the hall.

"Pay attention!" a man's voice barked. Heads whipped around to follow the sound. Zed looked over just in time to see Celia's hands fling back to her shield, which had been propped up casually against her knees, but it was too late: a dodo had discovered her weak link in the shield barrier and pecked at the gap, which sent her shield clattering to the ground. The dodo barged past her legs as she darted to retrieve it, and three of its friends decided to tag along.

Celia's father and a woman on her other side scooted in to cover the gap. The ushers managed to shoo the rest of the flock along, but the four fugitive birds had already strutted up the hall and around a corner.

"You better go fix your mess!" Celia's father barked again.

Her entire face flushed like an embarrassed tomato. Celia scrambled to her feet and dashed up the hallway.

Tuesday thought about leaving Celia to deal with the consequences of her carelessness alone. She even started thinking up the perfect insult to hurl after her. Turns out dodos aren't so harmless after all, huh Celia? But then she had a better idea. Why settle for putting a bully in her place, when Tuesday could rescue her instead? That'd show her who's pulling their weight around here!

"Come on!" Tuesday said to Zed and Fariq. She snatched up her shield and ran after Celia.

Fariq nodded silently at Zed. Zed nodded grimly back. They picked up their shields and followed the girls.

A trail of feathers (and Tuesday's shouts) led them to a nook where the corridor dead-ended at the back door to the kitchens. Tuesday and Celia had managed to corner the dodos with their shields, but now they faced the dilemma of taking them back. The dodos were far too big to pick up and carry. And there was nothing to use as a net, cage, or leash…

Zed pulled some jerky from his pocket and held it out for the nearest bird to try.

"What are you doing?" Tuesday shrieked.

"I thought we could use food to lure them back to the poultry wing. Maybe instead of having to chase them, they'd just follow us."

Celia wrinkled her nose at him. "What *is* that stuff, anyway?"

"Jerky," said Zed.

"*Dodo* jerky," Tuesday reminded him. "What are you trying to do, make cannibals out of them? They're unnatural enough as it is—don't give them any weird ideas!"

"Looks like they have a taste for *you* already," Zed shot

back as one of the birds snapped its beak at Tuesday's fingers. "Jerky was worth trying, at least."

"Dodos don't eat meat," Fariq commented blandly. "They like fruit."

"So go get some!" the girls shouted.

Zed shuffled sideways past the makeshift dodo corral and eased the kitchen door open. No one turned as he poked his head inside; the cooks were too busy pulling massive trays of rolls out of the ovens and slicing up melons to notice.

Melons! He leaned in and grabbed a chunk of discarded rind from a bin against the wall. Most of the good stuff had already been cut away, but there were still a few fragments of the sticky orange flesh clinging on. It would have to do.

Zed ducked back through the door and tossed the rind to Fariq, who dangled it over the girls' heads. Four leathery faces whipped around. He waved it slowly back and forth. Eight beady yellow eyes followed it greedily.

"Nice birdies," Fariq whispered. "Come get the treat."

The dodos hopped up and down, flapping their useless wings, but Fariq held the prize just out of reach.

Tuesday and Celia pulled their shields away and hastily stood up to avoid being trampled. Fariq calmly led the birds back up the hallway like some dodo-wrangling pied piper. Celia and Tuesday rushed ahead to open the poultry wing door, and the fugitives followed Fariq inside.

It was almost like a parade, Zed noted.

DODOS
a summary of observations, by Zed

Apparently, not as extinct as people think.

FEATHERS: very fluffy, color somewhere between gray and a dusty brown. (There should really be a name for this. Bray? Grusty? Needs work.)

TAIL: not much. A couple of curly feathers flop over.

SIZE: surprisingly big! I was expecting something in the turkey range, but these are the size of toddlers. Very fluffy, mean toddlers that bite.

CAUTION: no teeth, but beak is strong enough for a bite to cause bruising. Legs stumpy but strong. Can run surprisingly fast.

DIET: prefer fruit when they can get it. Didn't get a chance to test meat hypothesis, but they seem to keep sampling shins and fingers, so there might be something to this. Need more data.

CHAPTER 3
FIELD TRIP, INTERRUPTED

Celia never exactly thanked the others for their help, but after the dodo-wrangling escapade she was a bit nicer to them in class. There was less huffing and eye rolling, at least. And no more snide comments about Zed and Tuesday's family (though she probably wouldn't have made them with Professor Orpin in earshot anyway). By the end of the week she was acting positively cheerful. But then, it was easy to be in a good mood on field trip day.

Obviously they couldn't leave the base for this. Everyone living there had someone after them: The Legion's soldiers, the secretive Red Hand agents, or if someone in their family had *really* annoyed Falinnheim's tyrannical new government, both. Professor Orpin couldn't load everyone onto a school bus and spend the day touring a zoo or museum, or whatever passed for a semi-educational outing around here. So instead, school field trips took them through the duty stations at the base that were too specialized to offer rotating work assignments.

So far, Zed was really enjoying Professor Orpin's class. He appreciated the way the professor mentored each student individually, helping them choose projects and research assignments in their own areas of interest. Since the class covered students from ages eight all the way up to fifteen, it would have been pretty tough to get them all working on the same thing at the same time anyway. But all the same, Zed appreciated being asked what he wanted to learn, for a change. He felt like he was finally helping pilot his own education, instead of being stuck as a passenger.

Still, there was no denying that Professor Orpin could be a bit… *much,* sometimes. Zed had come to think of his teacher as a modern Ichabod Crane; aside from his long-limbed, gangly appearance, which looked a bit like someone had built a scarecrow out of noodles, the professor also had a habit of delivering long-winded speeches full of overly complicated vocabulary. Zed and Tuesday often joked that their teacher must spend his evenings raiding the thesaurus for spare parts. And his introduction to today's field trip was no different.

"This is an important step in your educational journey," said Professor Orpin, addressing the class in his usual pompous manner. "Remember, by age fifteen you will need to select an area of focus for your apprenticeship training. So in addition to comporting yourselves with dignity in a professional setting, I expect each of you to pay strict attention. Today may very well be the day you discover your life's vocation."

Linus—the youngest kid in the class—raised his hand. "What does 'comporting' mean? And 'vocation'? And 'dig—"

His older brother Dominic cut him off. "It means be good or they'll throw us out. And listen up, because you have to pick a job eventually, and it might be this one."

"Where are we going this time?" Oona wanted to know.

"We will be touring the Research and Development department," said Professor Orpin. "And the laboratory supervisor was quite specific about some of the hazardous things inside, so everyone keep your hands to yourselves, understood?"

"What kind of hazardous things?" asked Tuesday. "Acids? Explosives? Oooo! Maybe they have experimental weapon prototypes or something! I've been meaning to ask Captain Solomon about these sticky blobs I saw him use on those Red Hand agents that one time…"

"Will you at least *try* not to sound so excited about things that could land us all in the hospital wing?" Zed muttered to her.

"Hey, whatever's in there, it's *got* to be more exciting than our last field trip. I can't believe anyone would choose an apprenticeship in Geothermal Maintenance. It's just a bunch of tunnels and pipes! *Boring.*"

Zed had, in fact, considered learning more about the base's natural energy systems, but Professor Orpin silenced them all with a stern look and ushered the class into the hall, so Zed kept this to himself. Probably for the best anyway, he decided with a sigh. Tuesday would never let him hear the end of it.

After a brief procession through the maze of slick white hallways, the class filed into the laboratory. Tuesday and Zed had been here before, when the scientists wanted to study Nyx. Tuesday remembered the meeting with a grimace—the researcher leading the experiment had been obsessed with the idea of using Nyx as a weapon, and it had left a bad taste in her mouth about the whole department. She was just wondering whether the same unpleasant man would be leading the tour today when a familiar face answered the question for her.

"Hello," a young woman at the front of the room called. "Please gather over here by the tool dispensary so we can begin your tour."

Tuesday and Zed recognized her immediately. Though they'd had duty assignments with her several times since, they had first met Fatima on the very same day the scientists studied Nyx. She wasn't dressed in the typical blue uniform of the Support division today though, but a matching set of black tunic and trousers, something like a doctor's scrubs, covered by long white robes that resembled a lab coat. She had her hair wrapped up in a colorful scarf, as usual; today's selection was a bright magenta studded with teal polka dots.

"Hi, Auntie Fatima," said Fariq, waving at their guide. Fatima beamed and waved back.

"She's your aunt?" Tuesday asked.

"Yeah. My dad's sister."

Tuesday rolled her eyes. "I know what an aunt is, I'm just surprised you're related. You've never mentioned her before."

"I didn't know you knew each other," he said with a shrug.

Professor Orpin glared over at them and put a finger to his lips, but that didn't stop Linus from raising his hand. "What kind of science do you do?" he asked.

The professor glared some more, but Fatima was happy to indulge the boy's curiosity. "What a great question! The scientists working here have lots of different specialties. I work in what's called organizational science. I help people cooperate better in groups, study how groups with different responsibilities coordinate with each other, and design workspaces and routines that help people accomplish things more efficiently and feel good about their environments."

Linus raised his hand again.

Dominic sighed. "She helps people do good work and not argue," he explained, anticipating his brother's next question.

"No more questions right now," Professor Orpin

insisted. "Let's just start the tour."

"Right you are, Professor!" Fatima agreed cheerily. She cleared her throat and launched into her speech. "Welcome to Research and Development. The innovations designed and tested in this laboratory help make things easier all over the base. From the dental beads you use to clean your teeth every morning to the geothermal systems keeping the indoor temperature constant, lots of things you may take for granted as normal parts of your day were developed right here. Now if you'll follow me, I'll show you some of the equipment the scientists use to conduct their experiments."

Fatima guided them around the lab, pointing out microscopes and macroscopes, laser emitters and electrothermic scanners. Vials of colorful chemicals waited on workbenches next to bins of completely ordinary-looking rocks. It was something like getting a tour of Willy Wonka's workshop, but without the candy-bright color scheme and complete disregard for workplace safety. But after twenty minutes of gadgets whose names they couldn't remember and functions they couldn't even begin to guess, everyone's attention started to drift. Soon every head craned in a different direction, straining for another glimpse of whichever thing had caught their interest.

Fatima was deep into her explanation of the base's weather prediction algorithm when Zed elbowed Tuesday in the ribs.

"Watch it!" she hissed.

Zed gestured to the workstation behind them. "Look," he mouthed silently.

Tuesday followed Zed's stare, her grumpy expression dissolving the moment her eyes landed on a clear glass safety shield. Inside, a chain dangling from the ceiling suspended a big red hook. And hanging from the hook, folded up like a massive sleeping bat, was an ordinary-looking black umbrella. Their father's umbrella. The same one he'd used to defend them from the Legion's shape shifting swords during his dramatic rescue last fall. At least, Tuesday was pretty sure it was the same one. They'd have no reason to study a regular umbrella, right?

Tuesday raised her hand. Professor Orpin tried to silence her interruption with The Look all teachers have, but Fatima seemed pleased to be getting some student participation. "Yes, Tuesday, do you have a question?"

"What's that experiment for?" she asked, pointing over at the umbrella.

Fatima opened her mouth, but she never got to answer. Because at that exact moment, all the sirens went off.

CHAPTER 4
FIELD TRIP, EXTENDED EDITION

Flashing red lights emerged from the ceiling. All around the lab, researchers in white robes abandoned their workstations and hustled to the door. "All right, who touched something?" Professor Orpin shouted over the blaring.

The laboratory supervisor hurried over to them, the same man who'd inspected Nyx last fall. "It's not a lab safety warning!" he yelled back. "Sirens are going off all over the base. There's been a security breach!"

The professor's face went even paler than usual. He looked around wildly, trying to decide what to do. The lab supervisor rushed off to evacuate the scientists. The first two were nearly to the exit when a curtain of connected metal slats unfurled from the ceiling above the doorway and clanked to the floor. When the entire doorway was covered, the slats locked into each other to form a solid barrier. They were trapped.

Fatima jumped into action. "Quickly, everyone to the storage room! There's an emergency exit behind the fume hoods."

Professor Orpin nodded weakly and started herding kids behind her. The researchers who'd been stopped at the door wheeled around and followed her too.

Zed wasn't sure what made him do it. At first, he passed right by the workstation, obediently following Fatima to the exit. But then he stopped in his tracks and doubled back to look at the umbrella.

"What are you doing?" Tuesday yelled. "We've got to go!"

Zed looked at the shielded corner, then back at Tuesday. The lab was entirely deserted now—everyone was too busy escaping to notice any stragglers.

"Come on!" Tuesday urged. "What if the emergency exit seals too? We'll get stuck in here!"

Zed crouched under the glass hood and grabbed the umbrella.

———

If Zed had ever wondered what it felt like to be a dodo, he didn't have to wonder any longer. Being ushered with the jostling crowd through narrow passages must have been exactly like taking a spot in the poultry parade. Except instead of being herded toward the safety of their familiar coop, the panicked jumble of kids and lab workers were running *away* from home, chased by the specter of a threat no one had really yet explained.

The exit in the storage room had been a hatch in the floor, which swung up to reveal a slide that dumped them into a dimly lit bare room. Glowing crystals jutting through the rough stone walls formed large arrows pointing down a passageway only wide enough to allow two people to walk side by side. They snaked through the tunnel (Was it five minutes? Twenty? More?) until it ended in an identical stone room, except this one also had a huge metal panel set into the far wall, and a security monitor next to a big red button.

"How's it look out there?" asked the lab supervisor.

Fatima squinted at the screen. She toggled a tiny switch below it, and the view rotated to show the scenery in all directions.

Rocks. Scraggly, yellowed winter grass. A few slushy pockets of last week's snow that hadn't quite melted yet. "All clear, Penn," she reported. "Looks cold, though."

Zed surveyed the group from the back of the room. Luckily everyone was wearing shoes, since they'd been at work or school before the evacuation, but that also meant they were dressed in their uniforms for those tasks: the researchers in their black tunics and white robes, and the students in their light blue tunics and trousers. If Fatima was suggesting their next destination was outside, it was going to be a pretty chilly trip.

"Where are we even going?" Celia demanded. "What were all the alarms about, anyway?"

"Weren't you paying attention?" said Dominic. "There was a security breach."

"Yeah, but what's that *mean?*" Levi wanted to know.

"Will somebody please explain what happened?" called Lydia.

Professor Orpin was too busy hyperventilating to answer his students' questions. One of the researchers standing nearby suggested he sit down before he fainted— the last thing they needed was a medical emergency in the middle of an evacuation.

Supervisor Penn waded to the center of the crowd so he wouldn't have to yell. "Apparently someone who isn't supposed to be here got through one of the exterior doors to the base. And if the security team thought it necessary to sound the alarm, that means they couldn't stop them, so it was probably a *lot* of someones."

Linus raised his hand. Dominic pushed it back down.

"I still don't understand," Naomi whispered as she hugged her best friend, Sakura.

"It means," said Fatima heavily, "the Resistance is under attack."

Kids immediately started freaking out. Oona asked Professor Orpin where the younger class was scheduled to meet today, and if that meant her little sister had been evacuated too, or if she was locked inside the base with the intruders. Professor Orpin, whose face was now tinged the same gray-green shade as a dead fish, didn't look like he heard her. He looked more like he was about to get reacquainted with his breakfast. Naomi and Sakura were still hugging, but now they were crying as well. Linus tugged on his brother's sleeve and shout-whispered that he needed to go to the bathroom.

Even Tuesday, who usually resorted to false displays of aggression during a crisis, looked a bit rattled. "The security team couldn't stop them?" she said in disbelief. "But that means…"

Zed grabbed Tuesday's hand and gave it a silent, supportive squeeze. He understood: the security team meant Dad. Was he hobbling around right now, trying to fight off intruders despite his injured foot? Or had those barriers that sealed the lab door come down everywhere else too, trapping him wherever he'd been when the alarm sounded? Zed looked down at the stolen umbrella still clutched in his fist. Wherever Dad was and whatever he was doing, he was doing it without his weapon. Mom would be fine—no matter where she'd ended up, Nyx was sure to be with her. And neither the Legion's brutish soldiers nor the Red Hand's calculating agents had made it past the Gabriel Hound's defenses yet. But Zed was sure of one thing: his parents would not have evacuated the base unless they were sure everyone else made it out first.

A woman in white robes cleared her throat. "If the base

is full of intruders, they'll figure out how to get past the barriers eventually. We can't just wait here."

"Yes, what's the plan?" called the man next to her.

Penn elbowed his way to the front and turned to face the crowd. "The General's evacuation protocol states we should head to the nearest Resistance safe house and wait. Any Operations teams conducting missions in the area will meet us there."

"And then what?" shouted a researcher at the back.

"I *don't know*, okay?" Penn ran his fingers through his sandy brown hair and let out a slow breath, collecting his composure before he spoke again. "I don't know any more about what's going on than the rest of you. But Miel is right—we can't stay here and wait for the invaders to dig us out. Let's start with the instructions we have. We'll head to the safe house and see who else turns up. Then we can pool everyone's information and decide what to do next."

He nodded to Fatima, who smacked the red button next to the view screen. The metal panel slid open, disappearing sideways into the wall like an elevator door. Tuesday stood on her tiptoes, trying to catch a glimpse of whatever was behind it, but all she could see from the back of the room was a bright glare. She and Zed shuffled forward with the rest of the crowd until everyone else had funneled through the exit.

"—sixteen, seventeen, eighteen," Fatima counted, pointing at Zed, Tuesday, and then herself. She plucked three hooded cloaks off a row of metal hooks lining the passageway and handed two of them over for the kids while pulling on her own. Then she led them along the narrow hallway, up a ladder, and out a hatch disguised as a rock into the field outside.

"Everybody here?" asked Penn.

Fatima gave him a thumbs-up. "Eleven students, Professor Orpin, and the six of us," she confirmed, gesturing at the other scientists.

Penn pulled a clear glass sphere out of his cloak's pockets and held it in his palm, consulting it like a fortune teller searching for answers in a miniature crystal ball. He rotated on the spot, his head flicking up and down as he compared whatever information the ball was giving him with the landscape.

"This way," he said at last, striding confidently through the tall meadow grass. A line formed behind him as the evacuees followed him away from the foot of the mountain.

Tuesday leaned over to whisper to her brother. "I have *got* to get me one of those."

CRYSTAL BALLS?
(Not sure what they're actually called)
by Zed

Round clear glass people look into to get more information about stuff. Small enough to keep in a pocket. Fits into the palm of a hand—about the size of a plum.

To use: put it in your palm and look in it. Or look *at* it, I guess? You don't have to bring it close to your eye, you just hold it out.

Questions: How do they work? What are they for? Do all adults have them, or are they special?

- Fatima had one the first time I met her—used to tell time to make sure Nyx wasn't late for her appointment at the lab.
- A Resistance agent used it to record a video of interviewing Scrimbley. Then he gave it to the General, who showed the video to us. (Note: need to come up with better name options for General Grandma. This is getting really awkward.)

> - Lab leader already had one with him when he
> evacuated. It gave him directions to the safe
> house (somehow, I couldn't see how he used it.)
> Did it act like a compass? Did it show a map?
> Need more data.
>
> Hypothesis: something like a cell phone? But
> without the "phone" part. If we could call the
> base with it, we'd know what was going on.

Blaring alarms and anonymous intruders aside, it was kind of fun tromping through the meadow, drinking in the weak winter sunshine, puffing out steamy breaths like human tea kettles. After being stuck in an underground bunker for months, any chance to get outside was a treat. But after an hour of walking, the charm of the great outdoors started to wear off.

"Looks like we're getting a field trip today after all," said Levi, pulling his shoe out of a muddy patch with a wet squelch. "I could do with less of the *field* part though."

"Ugh, I've had enough of the *trip* part," complained Lydia, pulling her hood tighter around her ears. "I'm freezing! And my feet hurt. How much longer do we have to keep walking?"

"Quit whining!" said Celia. "Would you rather be trapped inside the base with the bad guys?"

Oona sniffled. "At least if we were at the base we'd

know what was going on. If the tunnels connected rooms to each other instead of to the outside, we could have met up with our families."

"She means her little sister," Fariq explained, even though no one asked. "They're not in the same class, so they got separated."

Dominic rolled his eyes. "Some people have all the luck."

Linus was busy tugging at his brother's cloak, trying to point out a boulder on the other side of the field that sort of looked like it had a face. Dominic was busy pretending not to notice. He also had to pretend he'd gone deaf, or forgotten his name, because the tugging was accompanied by a chorus of, "Hey! Hey, Dom! Look! Look over there, Dominic!" When that didn't work, Linus darted in front of his brother, waving his arms. Which caused Dominic to stumble into him, landing them both in a pile of snowy slush.

Zed braced himself for the older boy to start yelling, or the younger one to start crying. But incredibly, Linus dissolved into giggles instead.

"What's so funny?" his brother demanded.

Linus was laughing so hard he gave himself hiccups. "Field—*hic*—trip!" he explained when he caught his breath. "Get it? We're in a—*hic*—field, and we tripped. Field trip!"

Dominic scowled. But only for a moment. By the time he finished brushing off his cloak, his brother's comical sputtering got the better of him, and he found himself laughing right along with everyone else.

If the rumbling in Tuesday's stomach was any indication, it was nearly lunchtime when they caught their first glimpse of the safe house. At least, she assumed that's why all the adults were staring at the building sprouting from the weeds. It looked like nothing more than a ramshackle old cabin to her, just a collection of weathered wooden boards peeking from a copse of naked trees at the meadow's edge.

Penn stopped walking so abruptly Professor Orpin bumped into him. "Wait here," he said, slipping the glass ball back into his pocket. "I'll go ahead to check it out."

Fariq tucked his hand into Fatima's while they waited for the lab supervisor to return. "Just a precaution," she told him. "I'm sure everything will be fine."

"Auntie?" he asked after a moment of silent thought. "What should we do if everything's not fine?"

Fatima shrugged. "Go in and rescue him, I guess."

Celia let out an annoyed sigh. "Things are already *not fine*, in case you all forgot. That's why we're even here."

Everything was fine. Penn was only gone a minute or two before he snuck back to their hiding place and led them into the cabin. From the outside, the safe house was designed not to draw attention. It looked tiny. Old. Abandoned. Possibly haunted. As Zed and Tuesday got their first glimpse of the inside, they realized this was no illusion—it actually *was* old and tiny. (The jury was still out on the "haunted" part.)

The cabin's rough wooden door squealed on bent, rusty

hinges to reveal a single room of the same splintery boards, empty except for a fieldstone fireplace. There was barely room for everyone to stand, let alone live here until help arrived. Assuming help was coming at all.

Penn edged his way over to the fireplace. He pushed in one of the protruding stones, and the entire left side of the hearth swung forward like a door. Where the chimney should have met the floor, instead a set of metal stairs descended into a hidden basement. The moment Penn's foot hit the first step, rows of crystal light bulbs tucked between the cabin's floor joists blinked to life.

Everyone lined up behind Penn and followed him down the stairs. When the last person made it to the bottom of the staircase, the secret door closed automatically behind them. The basement was also a single open room, but unlike the cramped cabin above, this one was the size of a tennis court. The floor and walls were coated with the same slick white material as the hallways at the base. Two walls were lined with purple-cushioned benches; the other two had a simple kitchen area with a stove set into a long countertop, a collection of shelves scattered with barrels and crates, and a set of three identical doors.

One of the scientists, a portly man with a bristly gray mustache, put his hands on his hips and looked around with satisfaction. "This might not be so bad after all."

And that was when they heard the cabin's front door slam shut.

CHAPTER 5
UNEXPECTED
COMPANY

All the lights went out. Slivers of daylight fell through the cracks between the floorboards above, just enough for Zed and Tuesday to make out the panicked faces around them.

Sakura whispered to Naomi. "I *knew* this place was haunted!"

"Quiet!" Penn put a finger to his lips, pointed at the ceiling, and motioned for everyone to sit down. Normally telling a room full of kids to stop talking is an excellent way to get them all talking about how everyone should stop talking, but something about the way Penn said it stole their voices like all the air had been sucked from the room. Students and scientists alike, everyone crouched to the floor and looked up. Showers of dust sprinkled from the slatted ceiling, raining down wherever someone stepped on the cabin's main floor.

Heavy bootsteps. Creaking floorboards. Snatches of

mumbled conversation. Then the fireplace hatch swung open, sending a column of light spilling down the stairs. Whoever had opened it waited on the top step, holding out a glass ball; instead of acting like a watch or a map, this one was lit up like a flashlight. Tuesday threw a hand up to shield her eyes from the glare.

"Well, what do we have here?" The man's voice sounded amused. "Corvus, I think we may have mice in the cellar."

"Rabbits, more like," said a second man. "Awfully big footprints for mice. And who knew rabbits traveled in packs? They left a trail to the front door a blindfolded bat couldn't have missed."

Stupid! Tuesday thought. How could they have been so stupid? Whoever raided the base would have expected people to try to escape. Had the Legion been spying on them all morning, waiting for their chance to locate a Resistance safe house and round up additional captives in the bargain? No… the thuggish soldiers weren't patient enough for that. It was the Red Hand who watched and waited, striking like vipers when their victims least suspected it. Unless they were working together? The thought of their combined brute force and calculated cunning made her stomach do backflips.

Zed's mind was racing too, but toward an entirely different finish line. Something about the first man's voice sounded… *familiar.* Was this a soldier they'd bumped into before? He was so busy scouring his memory that he almost didn't notice Fariq stand up next to him.

The boy shuffled across the flashlight beam to the opposite wall and flicked up the light switch. "It's okay," he said as everyone blinked and shielded their eyes again. "It's only—"

"Captain Solomon!" Fatima exclaimed, her voice flooded with relief. "What are you doing here?"

Solomon smiled down at her from the top of the stairs. He switched off his light and handed the crystal ball to the man behind him. "We've been conducting an operation in Anduvia for three days now. The crew got tired of field rations, so we came back for more supplies. The question is, what are *you* doing here?"

Before any of the adults could explain, Linus piped up. "We're on a field trip."

Solomon and the other man burst into laughter. "You certainly are," said Solomon. "Come on, let's make some lunch and you can tell me all about it."

The first odd thing Zed noticed was that the agent thumping down the stairs after Solomon was much older than the captain. If the man's grizzled beard and shaggy, graying hair were any indication, he must be around the same age as the General. (Grandma? No, that still sounded weird.) Zed was used to the hierarchy in schools and businesses depending on experience, and usually that meant age. It was weird to see this gruff, hulking agent taking orders from Captain Solomon, who looked to be about his parents' age. Equally odd was the jagged purple scar snaking down from the man's left eyebrow, over the bridge of his lumpy, pockmarked nose, across his right cheek, and continuing down his neck. His left eye was the same blue-gray as the winter sky outside; the right one was a tawny brown. But the oddest thing of all was the massive black bird perched on his shoulder. It held so still Zed would almost have suspected it was fake, except he was pretty sure he saw it blink. Also, it would be even weirder to walk around with a fake bird on your shoulder than a real one.

The man swaggered into the cellar like some kind of goth pirate and removed his tattered gray cloak, revealing a strange collection dangling from a wide leather belt: a sheathed knife as long as his forearm, a set of night vision goggles, a corked waterskin, and a skein of mustard-colored yarn. The bird hopped onto his head as he whipped off the cloak, then shuffled back to his shoulder.

Penn scrambled off the floor. He tried to launch into explaining the raid and their evacuation, but Solomon cut him off. "Please, no business yet. Let's just enjoy our food first."

"You don't understand," said the lab supervisor. "This is urgent! We have to—"

Solomon laid a hand on the man's shoulder. "I know you're anxious, my friend. You wouldn't be here if your day was going according to plan. But I've been living off jerky and nutritional supplements for the past week, and I won't be much help to you if I give myself indigestion by wolfing down my first real meal so we can get to work. We need to plan before we can act, and we're an hour's journey from the nearest Resistance outpost anyway. A few more minutes won't change things."

As promised, it took only a few minutes for Captain Solomon's agents to cobble together a meal. After resetting the hidden security system on the main floor, four more agents joined the gathering downstairs. A stout, powerfully built woman pried the top off a wooden barrel and started passing around apples. Two more women rolled a wheel of cheese as large as a car tire out of an adjoining cold room, then cut it into wedges using a long wire with wooden handles at either end. The bird man, Corvus, pulled a tray of mugs out of the pantry and started filling them from a water tap set into the kitchen wall. Even Solomon pitched in, pulling the cushions off the benches lining the walls and instructing the scientists on the proper stacking configuration to turn the wooden bases into a low table. He passed the cushions to Orion, a young Resistance agent Zed and Tuesday had met before at the base, who distributed them among the school kids to line up around the table. When everything was ready, they all sat cross-legged on the floor cushions, resting their elbows on the low bench table. There were no dishes besides the mugs, but Solomon insisted that was for the best; less washing up to do later.

Only when the last apple core had been tossed into the compost bucket did Solomon allow Supervisor Penn to fill him in on the morning's events. Then he leaned onto his elbows, steepling his fingertips together in thought. A long silence followed, broken only by the rustling of Corvus's bird preening its feathers.

"Orion," he said at last.

The young agent sat up straighter on his cushion and turned eagerly toward his leader. "Yes, Captain? Whatever you need, I'm ready!"

Solomon smiled. "Please help the children set up everyone's hammocks, then take them upstairs for a while and keep them entertained. The leadership team needs to discuss our options." He turned to address the rest of the table. "Department heads and anyone with level-seven security clearance or higher is welcome to stay. Everyone else, please head upstairs."

Orion looked like his birthday had been canceled. "But sir, I really think *all* the Operations agents should—"

"We will fill you in when we have formed a plan," said Solomon firmly. "Besides," he added, his voice softening, "I need someone dependable to keep a lookout and protect our guests, should we get any uninvited visitors. Unless Professor Orpin would prefer the honor? I don't want to tell him how to manage his own students."

The professor choked into his mug, then cleared his throat. "As the only representative of the education committee on hand, I should stay for the meeting, of course. Acting department head, you might say."

Solomon nodded. "Agreed, professor. Everyone else—dismissed."

———

Apparently, Fatima didn't have level-seven security clearance either, because she and Orion were the only adults excluded from the meeting. Orion slouched to the far end of the room and stomped on a round depression in the floor the size of a dinner plate, which caused a huge metal column to rise slowly from it until it met the ceiling. He showed the students how to pull retractable hammocks from slots in the column and latch the other end to iron rings protruding from the surrounding walls. When they were done, it looked like they had erected a massive pine tree, with three layers of green hammock boughs radiating from a center trunk.

"Shoes and cloaks need to stay on," said Orion, "in case we need to leave in a hurry. But if you have any other personal effects, you can choose a hammock to stash them in. There's a ladder set into the front side of the support beam if you need to reach the upper levels."

Of course they all wanted hammocks at the top of the tree. But there were eleven kids, and only eight hammocks on the third level. Levi suggested they sort things out with a game of Fox, Hunter, Sparrow (which turned out to be exactly like Rock, Paper, Scissors: Hunter traps Fox, Fox eats Sparrow, Sparrow poops on Hunter.) After several fierce rounds, Linus, Naomi, and Sakura reluctantly settled into hammocks on the middle tier. That meant most of the adults would be near the floor, but that was fine, Orion insisted—they were likely to be changing guard shifts all night anyway. Better to get in and out of bed without having to climb the ladder and crawl past sleeping kids.

Zed and Tuesday selected neighboring hammocks near the ceiling. Each one had a zipper running down its length. "So you can zip yourself in to sleep," Orion explained from the ground. "Keeps people from falling out, and the top acts like a built-in blanket."

Zed and Tuesday sat in their hammocks, swinging slightly, and watched the other kids practice zipping themselves into the giant green cocoons.

"Come along!" called Fatima. "We need to get upstairs and let the leaders have their meeting in peace."

When the last kid had descended the ladder and headed for the staircase out of the cellar, Zed slid the umbrella out from under his cloak.

"Why did you bring that thing anyway?" Tuesday whispered as she took her turn on the ladder.

Zed answered with a silent shrug. He wasn't really sure what had compelled him to steal it from the lab. No, not steal, he thought. *Rescue.* He couldn't let something important enough for the Resistance to study fall into the wrong hands. He was just preventing the bad guys from getting it. And besides, it sort of belonged to his family anyway. It wasn't stealing to keep Dad's prized possession safe for him.

"Hurry up!" said Orion. "I have to keep all you squirts together."

"Coming!" Zed called. He stashed the umbrella inside his hammock and zipped it closed.

———

At first, Orion refused to participate in any sort of entertainment. He was too busy, he said, keeping a lookout for intruders. But then Fatima started a game of Musical Shadows, and before long he had drifted away from the cabin's single grimy window to watch the action. Soon he was whistling and humming and dodging the floor's patches of sunshine with the rest of them. He nearly jumped out of his skin when Corvus opened the fireplace hatch to let them know the meeting was over and they could come back downstairs.

The bird on his shoulder made a kind of clicking sound at them, followed by a loud *CRONK*.

"Hush up, Fiona," scolded Corvus, reaching up a finger to ruffle the bird's chest feathers.

"Hush up," it repeated.

"Woah!" exclaimed Sakura. "I didn't know crows could talk!"

"She's not a *crow*," said Corvus, grimacing as though Sakura had used some vile insult. "Fiona's a raven."

"Is there a difference?" asked Naomi.

"Crows are a lot smaller, for one," he explained gruffly. "Travel in huge flocks, making a racket and splatting massive droppings wherever they roost. Nothing but a bunch of noisy gossips. Ravens are more independent, and smarter too. They like solving puzzles and have an incredible memory for faces. Fiona here has saved more missions than I can count—alerted me to approaching soldiers, even recognized a pair in disguise spying on a village we were passing through."

"You should teach her to say 'nevermore'," Tuesday suggested.

She was met by confused stares.

"You know," she insisted, "like in the poem?"

"I don't think Falinnheim knows about Poe," Zed whispered. "Nursery rhymes have got to be older than 'The Raven,' and they don't have those here either, remember?"

Thankfully, the awkward moment was interrupted when the rest of Solomon's crew came up the stairs, each toting a bulging canvas knapsack over their cloaks. The three women nodded silently to Orion as they passed him, then filed out the cabin door.

"Where are they off to?" Orion asked.

"The captain wants them to check on the other safe houses," Corvus explained. "If anyone else managed to escape from a different side of the base, they would have headed to whichever one was closest. If we make contact with any other evacuees, we can see if they know more about the situation inside the base than we do. And if we don't find anyone, that will give us an idea how many people are still trapped inside."

"Excellent," said Orion eagerly. "What's my assignment?"

Corvus arched an eyebrow at him. "I believe you've already got one, lad."

"Babysitting?" Orion's lip curled in disgust. "They've already got a teacher—why can't the professor watch them?"

Corvus dropped his voice to a soft growl. "Because the professor's about as sturdy under pressure as a bruised grape, and you know it. Now see to your duty, agent, or I'll report you for insubordination."

Fiona cocked her head and focused one beady black eye on Orion, as though daring him to argue. She craned around to keep staring the young agent down while Corvus thumped back to the hidden stairs.

When the lieutenant had ferried his pet out of sight, Orion turned to find Celia was now glaring at him too. "Nobody asked *us* if we wanted to be stuck with you either, you know. Nobody cares what we think about *anything*, in fact. And it's getting really old." Then she spun on her heel and started after Corvus.

Fariq watched in pensive silence as she stormed down the stairs. "She's worried," he observed. "Everyone else is too. But they're pretending not to be. So they're acting mad instead." He headed for the stairs too but paused on the first step. "Know what?" he added thoughtfully. "I like it when people tell the truth. It makes everything easier."

Fatima sighed. "They're not *lying,* it's just… a lot of

people aren't good at finding the right words for how they feel. And not everyone is as comfortable sharing their thoughts as you are."

Fariq considered this. "Sometimes I make people uncomfortable, too," he said with a shrug. "But ignoring uncomfortable things doesn't make them go away."

Fatima shook her head and followed her nephew down the stairs. "You're right, of course, Bug. I wish more adults remembered how to tell the truth."

Safe House Roll Call
by Zed

CLASS	SCIENTISTS	OPERATIONS TEAMS
-Professor Orpin	-Supervisor Penn	-Captain Solomon
-Celia (14)	-Neri	-Lieutenant Corvus
-Dominic (13)	-Skandar	-Bronwyn
-Tuesday (12)	-Miel	-Valis
-Oona (12)	-Dev	-Amira
-Fariq (11)	-Fatima	-Orion
-Zed (11)		
-Lydia (10)		Honorary Member:
-Levi (10)		-Fiona the Raven
-Sakura (9)		
-Naomi (8)		
-Linus (8)		

CHAPTER 6
SOLOMON'S STORY TIME

Downstairs, Captain Solomon stood in front of the supply shelves, counting boxes. He took a step back and frowned.

"Something wrong?" asked Penn.

Solomon sighed. "Safe houses are normally just a travel stop for agents on their way to a distant city, or a fallback option if something goes wrong with an intelligence operation. They're not designed to handle a mass evacuation. Even with Bronwyn, Valis, and Amira off checking on the other hideouts, we're going to be packed in here like sardines."

Now it was Penn's turn to frown at the sparsely filled shelves. "We can handle a few days of crowding. It's the supplies I'm worried about. Doesn't the Support division keep the safe houses stocked?"

"We were due for a resupply this week, but under the

circumstances, I wouldn't count on that. And it doesn't help that I had to send the reconnaissance team off with half of what's left. Operations teams keep a little money on hand, but not enough to buy groceries for this many people."

Linus came up behind them. "Whatcha talking about?"

Penn flinched like he'd been caught with his hand in the cookie jar, but Solomon smiled down at the eavesdropper. "Nothing to bother young ears with. What we *need* to be talking about is the plan for tonight."

The rest of the class drifted over. "Tonight?" asked Lydia. "What's tonight?"

Naomi's face lit up. "Yeah, I almost forgot! It starts on Providence fifty-first this year, doesn't it? That's today!"

Levi was smiling and nodding too, but everyone else looked mystified.

"What are you talking about?" said Tuesday.

"You may not be familiar with this tradition, since you're… *new* here," Solomon began, choosing his words carefully. He knew that Zed and Tuesday had arrived from another dimension, but that was classified information. "It's an ancient holiday celebrated by my people. But of course everyone is welcome to join the festivities, even if their families don't usually participate. We could all use a break—it's been a stressful day."

Great, Zed thought, another weird new celebration.

"You're going to love it," Naomi agreed. "It's one of my favorites. It's called Hanukkah."

"I actually know that one!" Zed exclaimed over the murmur of collective appreciation. "Some people in our last, uh… *village* celebrated Hanukkah too. But—" He paused, looking up into the captain's deep brown face. "I guess I'm surprised to hear you celebrate it. Most of them didn't—um, look much like you." He'd had a couple Jewish friends back home, but they looked more like Naomi: pale, curly-haired kids who said their great-great-grandparents came from Europe. He couldn't remember any Black kids ever talking about their Hanukkah plans.

Solomon didn't seem offended by this observation, Zed noted with relief. Just confused.

"What an odd thing to say. I know it's a tradition usually passed down in families, but—"

"Never mind," Zed interrupted. "I'm sorry—that *was* a weird thing for me to say. We'd love to spend Hanukkah with you."

———

Despite never having celebrated Hanukkah before, Tuesday and Zed thought they knew what to expect. They'd watched enough holiday TV specials to know about latkes and dreidels, presents and candles. It was like Christmas, they assumed, but stretched out over eight nights instead of a single morning. But apparently things were different in Falinnheim, because there wasn't a blue snowflake garland or wrapped present in sight.

Solomon split everyone into teams, slicing apples and

shelling nuts. Levi, who everyone agreed was the best artist in the class, helped Fatima sculpt a menorah out of some clay they dug from the field behind the cabin. Miel, one of the scientists, found a few beeswax candles in the cold-storage room. Soon the table was covered in steaming platters of food, and the enticing blend of aromas beckoned all the workers to their seats.

Solomon knelt on his cushion at the head of the table and raised his hands for silence. Tuesday assumed he was about to give a short welcoming speech, or maybe offer a prayer. But instead, he opened the celebration by telling a story.

"Our stories say our ancestors were travelers," he began. "Not to follow the herds or the seasons, as some groups did, but in search of a place they could live in peace according to their beliefs. Sometimes they found a promising place, only to be rejected by the groups that already lived there. Other times they began building homes, only to have outside invaders try to wipe them out or take over. In one of these times, our people had settled into a land for many generations—and then a new king came to power.

"This king tried to promote himself as the only leader the people could look to. He claimed that anything that made people different divided them, and the only way to have peace and unity was through sameness. He tried to force our people to replace their traditions and beliefs with his own. He invaded their sacred temple and erected a statue of Zeus. The king's soldiers killed anyone who resisted.

"Some people decided it was better to fit in than be killed. But others were determined to stand up to the evil king. They formed a resistance to fight for their lives, their religion, their culture, and their independence, led by a man called the Hammer. They were outnumbered, of course—fighting against professional soldiers who rode on huge mythical beasts with noses like serpents and feet like battering rams, with curved teeth as long as swords. So this resistance had to fight with strategy and cunning instead of brute force. They hid in caves in the mountains and carried out surgical strikes, capturing their enemies' supplies and harassing their every move like a swarm of mosquitoes. They learned that their victories didn't have to be swift or dramatic—it was enough to make their oppressors' daily tasks *difficult*. Day after day, they chipped away at the soldiers' confidence. And when the soldiers were tired and frustrated, they let their guard down, creating openings for more meaningful attacks.

"After years of struggle, the resistance finally managed to retake their temple. They cleaned out all the things the king had tried to change about it. The last step was to light the menorah, a flame which they believed should never be allowed to go out. Now in those days, they didn't have crystals for light as we do, or even candles; they had to burn oil. But they only found enough oil to burn for one night, and it would take them eight days to make more. It didn't seem like what they had to offer would be enough, but just like in their battles, they decided that trying against all odds was better than giving up. And then a miracle happened: the oil kept burning for eight days instead of one, giving them the time they needed to make more.

"Keeping a light burning might seem like a small, symbolic thing, but it gave the people what they needed: hope. Hope that when they felt outnumbered and powerless, when it seemed useless to keep trying, what little they had to offer could be enough after all. The war was not yet over, but the miracle inspired our ancestors to keep fighting." Solomon pulled one candle out of its place at the center of the menorah. He lit it with a match, then used that candle to light another one off to the side. "They learned that, like candles, one small flame of hope and determination can help light countless others."

Solomon finished his tale and settled into his cushion. For a moment, everyone just sat there, mulling over what they'd heard. Finally Dominic broke the silence. "Is this a true story?" he asked. "Did all that really happen?"

Solomon nodded.

Levi beamed. "That's just like us! Making a new home in the mountains and pestering the soldiers. Tyrren is trying to change everything, but we're not giving up. Our leader even has a secret nickname—the Green Fly."

"The Hammer sounds tougher, though," said Lydia.

"Some of those giant monsters would sure come in handy," Oona observed. "I bet Tyrren would pee his pants if we rode into Alexandria on a bunch of those!" She sighed. "We don't even have horses—only the Legion is allowed to use them."

Tuesday leaned over to whisper to Zed. "Had you heard of Hanukkah monsters before?"

"I'm not *totally sure*," he whispered back, "but I think they might mean elephants."

"They have dodos, but not elephants? This place is so weird."

Zed shrugged. If any of Falinnheim's wildlife could be called a monster, it would be Nyx, and they'd managed to pass her off as a regular dog for over a decade. Describing an elephant to someone who had never seen one would probably sound terrifying.

After the storytelling and the lighting of the menorah, it was finally time to eat. They didn't have a lot of ingredients on hand, but Solomon was able to devise some workarounds that came close to Falinnheim's traditional Hanukkah foods, even without milk, butter, flour, or spices. He had manned the stove himself, turning out dozens of fried cheese sticks coated in crumbled-up wayfarer's biscuits. Orion and Corvus sliced mountains of apples with their long knives, and a couple of the scientists whipped up a honey-based spread to dip them in, which doubled as an excellent glaze for the toasted hazelnuts. They'd even managed a thin stew by chopping up pieces of jerky and the last two shriveled potatoes into some boiling water.

Everyone snacked and talked and told jokes. After asking Corvus about Fiona's favorite foods, Dominic and Fariq started a competition to see who could get the raven to catch more of the tidbits they tossed to her without letting them hit the ground. Then Oona, Naomi, and Sakura devised some puzzles for her, testing whether the raven could work out how to extract bits of apple from overturned crates or mugs. Fiona seemed to be enjoying these games immensely, but everyone else soon discovered it was nearly as fun to watch as it was to play. Even Professor Orpin, who usually wavered between solemn dignity and nervous handwringing, was beginning to let his guard down and embrace the festive atmosphere. When Fiona worked out how to extract a bit of jerky from inside a handkerchief trussed up with a bootlace, he cheered and impulsively hugged the scientist standing next to him, completely abandoning his usual decorum.

Everyone was so engrossed in the festivities that at first, they didn't notice when the intercom crackled to life. "Quiet," the voice on the other end commanded. "Someone's coming."

"Hush up!" Fiona squawked.

The celebration died instantly. Everyone froze, barely daring to breathe, and turned to watch the staircase.

"Could be one of the reconnaissance agents coming back with news," Penn suggested.

"Better not take chances," Solomon whispered back.

"We'll know for sure in a second."

The fireplace hatch creaked open.

Thump. Thump. A pair of brown leather boots appeared on the top step. They moved down to the next step, revealing a baggy set of thick woven trouser legs. One step lower: a rounded form bundled in layers of cloaks and wraps.

A gravelly voice spoke. "You didn't start the party without me, did you?"

Tuesday turned to whisper to Zed. "Is that—?"

Zed grinned. "Yep!" He'd recognize that voice anywhere. But how had she managed to get all the way out here?

Apparently, Zed wasn't the only one who recognized the voice, because a dozen people exclaimed at once: "Obaachan!" Fatima sprang up to help her off the last step, but the old woman waved her off and pulled out the walking stick she'd tucked under her arm.

"I'll have to have a word with Skandar about proper guard-duty protocol," said Solomon, frowning. "He could have told us it was you."

Obaachan laughed. "Who, that man lurking in the upstairs window? He's too busy to bother with the intercom. I put him to work."

"Doing what?" asked Solomon.

"Unloading my sled, of course! Everyone wants to help an old lady walk around, but you think I'll be hauling around heavy crates all by myself?"

"Crates?" Penn repeated.

"CRATES. Yes, boy—crates. And I thought *my* hearing was bad, honestly. How else am I supposed to keep a month's worth of food from falling off a hoversled?"

Before the adults could stop them, Professor Orpin's entire class pelted up the stairs and out the cabin door. Outside, they found Skandar busily loosening the heavy twine securing dozens of wooden crates to the back of the largest hoversled they'd ever seen. The swift, lightweight models most villagers used had just enough room for three or four passengers to sit cross-legged behind the standing driver, but Obaachan's cargo delivery sled was the size of a bus. It wasn't hovering at the moment, but nestled into the tall, dry meadow grass outside the cabin's front steps.

The bright moon overhead cast a blue glow on the scene, reflecting off the silent snowflakes that were just beginning to fall. Snowflakes caught in everyone's hair and eyelashes as the children examined the bounty from all angles, gleefully calling out the labels stamped on the crates: sugar cubes and caramel toffees, dehydrated oats and powdered apple cider, flour and spices, dried fruits and fresh root vegetables, barrels of fragrant oranges and vats of salted butter. And not just food, either; there were bundles of woolen mittens and hats and scarves, stacks of carved wood serving platters, a collection of gleaming metal forks, and even a small, locked chest that, when shaken, made a cheerful clinking that sounded suspiciously like coins knocking together. Apparently even after all this shopping, Obaachan still had plenty of her budget to spare.

Naomi stood back and surveyed the winter wonderland, beaming. "Looks like we got a Hanukkah miracle of our own," she declared.

CHAPTER 7
THE INVISIBLE
DELIVERY SERVICE

When all the supplies were hauled downstairs and sorted, and Obaachan was settled into a bench with double layers of cushions with a cup of hot cider, she finally explained. Her day had started with an early-morning supply run to Kyoto. Ever since two soldiers were attacked in the village square, the Kyoto village council had added so much extra security on market days that the General hadn't thought it wise to let anyone from the Operations team show their faces in town. And the Support division leaders were all wanted fugitives, so they couldn't go out in public either. "But no one looks twice at a harmless old woman," Obaachan explained with a satisfied chuckle. "When I got back to the base, all the entrances were locked out, and no one answered the intercoms. So I headed back to the Kyoto safe house—no one there either."

Fatima couldn't have looked more pitiful if Obaachan had been reading a story about abandoned kittens shivering in a gutter. "So you've been traveling all day, all alone? How did you ever manage?"

Obaachan frowned at her. "Weren't you listening, child? I was on a hoversled with a month's worth of supplies—had everything I could possibly need right under my rump. I spent a lovely winter afternoon driving around in the sunshine. Around sunset, I stopped and had a picnic. Best outing I've had in ages."

"But weren't you worried?" asked Miel. "The Resistance is under attack! Who knows what's going on inside the base?"

She waved this concern away. "My daughter-in-law and grandson are in there, along with Falinnheim's rightful heir and a beast that crawled out of Tyrren's nightmares. They'll handle it. If you want someone to feel sorry for, it's the fools that thought they could take on the Resistance in their own house. Those punks will never know what hit them."

Zed wasn't so sure about that. He had run afoul of both the Legion and the Red Hand before, and neither had struck him as particularly helpless. No matter which of them had found a way in, Obaachan was treating ruthless, armed intruders as a mere annoyance, like discovering ants in the pantry. But since there was nothing he could do to help, for the moment he allowed himself to indulge in a little optimism.

***

Obaachan may have talked tough, but no one was willing to let a possibly-hundred-year-old woman onto a ladder. That was just asking for trouble. And besides, Corvus pointed out, all the hammocks were taken anyway. So Fatima and Orion pushed a couple of the benches together to form a bed for her, lined with every cushion they could find.

"Lights out in ten," Solomon called. "Professor, you and Penn are taking the first watch. Wake up Neri and Dev for their turn at midnight."

"You ducklings get a good night's sleep," Obaachan called from her bed. "We've got a big day tomorrow."

This was news to everyone, including the captain. "What's happening tomorrow?" Solomon asked, squinting suspiciously at her. On the hammock tree, heads popped up all over the upper branches.

"Our next operation, of course."

Solomon laughed, but it didn't strike Tuesday as a "what a great joke" kind of laugh. More like a "the thing you just said is so ridiculous I must have misheard you" laugh.

"I appreciate your enthusiasm," he said, "but half my agents are still off checking the other safe houses. I won't be making any new plans until they report back."

Now it was Obaachan's turn to laugh. "Good thing your agents aren't invited, then. I have a few plans of my own. Don't fret yourself, pigeon—the children and I will handle it."

"My Operations team is leading this—" he started, but Obaachan cut him off.

"Don't forget I outrank you," she said sternly.

Solomon and Corvus exchanged a glance. "Does she?" Corvus mouthed silently. Solomon shook his head.

"Call it seniority, then. Can't argue with me there!"

Solomon folded his arms. "And this plan involves the children *how*, exactly?"

"Well we can't exactly show up in Anduvia with a bunch of well-trained, *competent*-looking people, now can we? You'd have Tyrren's informants on your tail the moment you set foot in town. Obviously, this operation calls for a more specialized skill set."

Orion cut in, speaking slowly while his tongue caught up to his thoughts. It was like he was trying to puzzle out the answer to Q minus Purple. "You need the specialized skills... of people with no training whatsoever?"

"Exactly," said Obaachan, rolling over and fluffing her pillow. "You can't *teach* someone how to be invisible."

———

"One child on their own doesn't work," Obaachan lectured over breakfast the next morning. She stirred some extra raisins into her mug of porridge and took a moment to savor a spoonful of the steaming glop before going on. "A single child, or even two, seems like they might be lost. And three look like they're plotting mischief. Draws attention."

"I still don't see why the adults can't do this," Solomon protested. "If you insist on going yourself, at least take Corvus or Orion along for protection. And the children don't need to be involved at all."

Obaachan carried on like she hadn't heard him. "An old woman alone doesn't work either. Ruffians see an easy target. They'll be picking my pockets or trying to make off with my bag. And the nicer folks will insist on helping me step over curbs, or asking if I need directions. Still too much attention. But an old woman *with* a group of children—that's the magic combination. The children look innocent, but supervised. The adult looks harmless, but not vulnerable. No one will give us a second glance."

"But you said you go alone all the time, getting supplies for the base," Dominic reminded her.

"That was different. I actually *was* shopping at the market. It wasn't a spy operation. This one's going to require a lot more strategy."

"What about a couple of children with an agent?" Solomon bargained.

"People might suspect they're being kidnapped," Obaachan countered. "All your agents look too… capable. Like they're up to something. No, it has to be me."

Solomon was practically begging now. "An adult who's *not* an agent then," he insisted. "Professor Orpin, or one of the scientists."

Hearing his name, the professor blanched six different shades of pale and concentrated on his porridge. But Obaachan wasn't willing to consider him anyway. "Too guilty-looking," she declared. "He's about as calm under pressure as a squirrel trying to cross the street."

"I'd be happy to go with you," said Fatima.

Obaachan actually paused a moment before announcing her judgment this time, peering along the table to consider her latest volunteer. "Nope," she said at last. "Too pretty. We're trying to make people ignore us, not stroll through the market turning heads."

Fatima blushed at this, but for some reason, so did Orion. Zed stared alternately between them, trying to decipher the odd interaction, but he didn't make any progress before the next interruption.

"What are we even *doing*?" Levi wanted to know.

"We've got to get the word out to all our allies," said Obaachan. "Village recruiters, undercover palace agents, the whisper network… there are lots of people on our side who wouldn't have a reason to show up at a safe house. If the Resistance is under attack, we've got to gather whoever's left and strike back."

"I don't disagree with you there," said Captain Solomon. "Even if we don't have a plan yet, we need to put our informants on alert. But they're spread all over Falinnheim. How are we going to get the word out to that many people without getting caught?"

Obaachan rolled her eyes. "We're going to order some eggs, of course."

———

In the end, Obaachan got her way, but everyone had to make a few compromises. Fariq pointed out that teenagers were as likely to be suspected of mischief as a trio of unsupervised children, so Celia and Dominic got cut from the excursion team. Dominic insisted his brother wasn't going anywhere without him, so Linus reluctantly agreed to stay behind too. Solomon put his foot down; he refused to authorize the mission unless they had backup. He assigned Orion and Corvus to head to the village market before the kids arrived and keep an eye on them from a safe distance, just in case anything went wrong. Obaachan agreed, but only because she thought they'd make an excellent decoy, drawing any soldiers' attention to themselves and away from her.

After breakfast Obaachan bundled up in her cloaks and wraps and headed out into the crisp winter morning. She settled herself on an empty crate behind the hoversled's control panel and waited for the kids to sit on the floor behind her. When everyone was ready, she pushed a button, which brought the sled humming to life, rising a half meter off the thin layer of snow that had fallen during the night.

"Sit tight!" she called. Then the sled lurched forward, following the meadow path to the village of Anduvia.

Anduvia's market looked much the same as the one Zed and Tuesday visited months ago, on their first day in Falinnheim. After parking the sled at the edge of town, Obaachan led everyone to a large square clearing in the village center, where they found cobblestone streets packed with haggling shoppers. Vendors called out rhyming jingles to entice shoppers to their stalls piled with blankets, or shoes, or fresh-baked pastries. Though it was the middle of winter, there were fruits and vegetables in abundance. There were even live animals for sale; at one stall Zed was amused to notice a couple of dodos pecking at the latch to their pen and jealously eyeing all the mangos, melons, and berries on the table next to them. But Obaachan led them past all these tempting curiosities and up to a dignified brick storefront on the next street over. CORDELIA'S APOTHECARY, the sign read, CONSULTATIONS BY APPOINTMENT.

Obaachan clanked the brass knocker on the faded black door and hummed tunelessly to herself until the door opened. "Good morning," she said to the woman regarding her suspiciously from behind the door. "I'd like to place an order for some eggs. About three dozen should do it, I think."

"You must be mistaken," the woman replied. "This is an apothecary. I sell ingredients for soaps and medicines, not produce. I'm sure you can buy eggs from one of the vendors at the village market."

For a dark, fleeting moment, Tuesday was actually worried. What if this whole plan was based on nothing but the ramblings of a confused old woman? Or maybe this shop had been home to one of their allies a decade ago, and Obaachan didn't realize how much time had passed since her last visit. But Obaachan wasn't deterred in the least. "Oh, I'm sure there's more to your inventory than meets the eye," she insisted. "Perhaps I can commission a special order—something outside your *general* customers' interest."

The shopkeeper must have been satisfied Obaachan wasn't a spy, because when she heard the word "general" she stood aside to let them enter. Then she led them through a waiting room, past the sales desk, and into another room at the back. Once everyone filed inside, she closed and locked the door behind them. She didn't ask Obaachan why she had a bunch of kids in tow; she just retrieved a wooden bucket from under the long worktable against one wall.

"What's the message?" she asked, carefully setting the bucket down next to her as she took a seat at the table. She twisted the crystal into place in the lamp dangling overhead, flooding her workspace with warm, pink-tinged light.

Obaachan didn't even have to think about it. "Base breached," she recited. "Collective action imminent. Await further instructions."

The woman dutifully punched this message into a touchscreen monitor set into the wall above the table.

Then, like a cash register spitting out a receipt, it produced a long, thin strip of paper with the message printed on it. When it finished printing the message, a blade flicked down to cut the strip loose before repeating the same printing on the remaining roll. In a couple of minutes a neat stack of identical messages built up on the workbench.

Everyone huddled around behind the woman's chair to see what would happen next. She took the lid off the bucket and pulled out what appeared to be an ordinary chicken's egg. A sharp, pungent scent wafted from the open bucket, which was filled to the brim with more eggs submerged in some kind of clear liquid.

"What's that smell?" Lydia asked, wrinkling her nose.

"Vinegar," the woman replied. "I always keep a supply of eggs soaking and ready to go."

Obaachan leaned on her walking stick and offered the woman a crisp, satisfied nod, as if this was the only sensible thing to be doing with a massive bucket of top-secret eggs.

The woman retrieved a scalpel from the workbench drawer. Cupping the egg gently in her hand, she made a tiny slit in the top. To everyone's surprise, the egg did not shatter; the shell had the slightest bit of give to it, like it was made of leather instead of brittle calcium. She took one of the messages off the stack, folded up the slip of paper, and forced it through the gap and inside the egg.

"I'll need to soak these for at least an hour," the woman said, turning to Obaachan. "Cold water firms the shells right back up. The slit will seal itself, and no one will know you're carrying anything more interesting than groceries."

"Perfect," Obaachan said. "We have more supplies to buy at the market anyway. We'll be back to collect them after our shopping."

"Shopping" turned out to mean even more eggs. After wading back into the crowded square, their first stop was at a stall selling trays, tote bags, and hats woven out of river reeds. Obaachan dug a wire loop from her cloak pocket and counted off the copper coins strung on it, handing the shopkeeper three hours in exchange for thirty-six baskets. She passed everyone four baskets, then proceeded to a farmer's stall, where they purchased nearly two hundred eggs to distribute between them. After this, Obaachan insisted on stopping to ogle at every interesting hat she spotted along the way and compliment the handiwork of all the silversmith's spoons. Then at last it was back to the apothecary, two baskets dangling off of every arm, wading gingerly through the crowd to avoid jostling the eggs.

The woman let them in without a code phrase this time and reported that all the eggs with messages inside had hardened nicely. One by one, she retrieved them from the bucket of cold water waiting behind the sales desk, dried them on her apron, and placed one egg in each of the kids' baskets. She was right, Zed noted—they blended in perfectly. No one would ever suspect there was anything unusual going on, especially since each altered egg was nestled in with five completely identical decoys.

Obaachan bought a bottle of cloudberry poultice as a cover for visiting the shop, and then it was back out into the crowded market. "Good thing I've got all you pigeons to help carry these eggs," she chuckled as they elbowed their way past the bundled-up shoppers. "We have a lot of deliveries to make."

A man passing in the opposite direction bumped her slightly, but not enough to break the eggs or make her trip. "Pardon, ma'am," he mumbled, pulling his scarf tighter around his face.

"Not so fast." Obaachan stuck her walking stick out in front of him, whapping the man across the knees. "I'll take that back now."

He tried to step around her. "I don't know what you—"

"Don't play coy, lad," she insisted. "Give it back, or I'll send old Shinbiter here somewhere you won't soon forget."

Corvus and Orion appeared on either side of her. "Is there a problem, madam?" Corvus growled, staring the man down with the quiet intensity of a guard dog. Fiona, perched on his shoulder, cocked her head, training one beady black eye on the man too.

"I've got it under control, young man," said Obaachan, playing along as though she didn't know them. "Slight misunderstanding. It seems one of my eggs accidentally jumped into his man's pocket."

Without another word, Corvus and Orion seized the man by the shoulders and whisked him off to the nearest alley. Fiona flapped around the thief's head, pulling down his hood and plucking at the woolen scarf wrapped around his face.

"Search him," Corvus ordered. As he turned the man around to pin him to the wall, Fiona finally pulled the last of the scarf free, revealing a weather-beaten face sporting graying stubble and a guilty smile.

Tuesday almost dropped her baskets. "*Scrimbley?* What are *you* doing here?"

CHAPTER 8
EXTRAORDINARY EGGS

"You know this thief?" Corvus still had Scrimbley by the collar, holding him still while Orion searched all the hidden pockets in his cloak. He dumped a broken alarm clock, three forks, a ball of purple yarn, and an apple with two bites already missing into the street before finally locating the stolen egg.

"We've met," said Tuesday with a scowl. Corvus released his grip, but he and Fiona kept their sights locked on Scrimbley.

"What do you want an egg for, anyway?" Zed asked him.

Scrimbley shrugged. "Professional habit. My hands gets a mind to themselves, now and then. Just happen to rescue anything that looks as it's not being tended proper."

"A week in Anduvia's jail would tend *you* proper," Obaachan scolded. "Luckily for you we have more errands to run.”

“All’s well that ends well,” Scrimbley agreed, brushing off his cloak. “Got places to be, myself. I’ll be on my way, then.”

“Wait a minute,” Orion protested, blocking the thief’s retreat. “We’re just letting him get away with this?”

Obaachan laughed. “Well we can’t exactly call the village patrol, now can we?”

“’Course not,” said Scrimbley. “Wouldn’t want to waste their time over something as simple as an ordinary egg. Unless…” he added, eyeing the cluster of basket-toting kids, “it’s no ordinary egg after all? It’s not every day you see a grocery delivery with its own private security goons.”

Orion loomed so close his breath fogged Scrimbley’s face. “Meaning *what*, exactly?”

Scrimbley didn’t even flinch. “You folks don’t strike me as being too friendly with the village patrol yourselves,” he said quietly. “Saw a couple soldiers loitering across the square. Could be they’d offer to settle matters for us. Might be real keen to meet a couple of your young helpers in particular.” He flashed a sideways glance at Zed and Tuesday.

Zed thought Scrimbley had an excellent point. Even if the soldiers assigned to this village didn’t recognize them, getting the Legion involved while they were smuggling secret messages was a pretty big risk, especially over something as trivial as a failed pocket picking. But before Orion could answer him, Tuesday jumped in.

"Speaking of friendly," she said, pasting on her most charming smile, "I never got to thank you for your help with our friends. You know, the ones you invited to my house a few weeks ago? I'm sure my dad would like a chance to thank you, too. I'll be sure to mention we bumped into you."

For the first time, Scrimbley looked flustered. "Your father? I… he…" He gulped. "I'm sure he's real busy. No need to bother him. Simple misunderstanding."

Obaachan was getting impatient. "We don't have all day to stand around chatting. You boys can settle this without us." She started down the street, trailing a line of basket-toting kids behind her. "And check your pockets," she called over her shoulder. "While you were busy searching him, the scoundrel lifted both your coin rings."

––––––––––

The deliveries took the rest of the morning. Obaachan led them all over the village, stopping at a barber shop, a bakery, several farms, and a blacksmith's forge. Sometimes she handed over one basket of eggs, smiling and chatting about the weather like she was delivering a gift to an old friend. But on their final stop, the dispatch office, she played the part of a customer arranging deliveries, and left two dozen baskets with instructions to distribute them to contacts in other villages. One basket was even destined for the kitchen at Tyrren's palace.

"Are you sure that's a good idea?" Oona asked as they hovered down the deserted meadow path to the safe house. "What if the wrong person cracks open the egg? If they're not on our side, they might tell Tyrren—he'd find out about the plan before it even got started."

"What plan?" Tuesday grumped. "It's been a whole day since the base got invaded, we still don't know what's going on, and no one's decided what to do if we ever figure it out."

Obaachan turned around in surprise. "Weren't you listening? At every stop in the village, I asked our contacts what they know about the raid. We learned quite a bit. We have lots of news to take back to the captain."

"We do?" Levi asked. "What news?"

"So all that talk about whether it's going to snow soon and how people's kids are doing—that must have been code!" Zed realized. "But what did it mean?"

"If you weren't paying attention, I'm not going to repeat it," Obaachan replied. "And don't worry about the deliveries. Our allies will make sure they get into trusted hands. We've had undercover agents working in the palace for years. The kitchen staff know to be picky about who gets to make omelets."

"Wow," said Lydia. "Working right under Tyrren's nose without getting caught? Those must be some *cracking* good spies!"

There was a chorus of groans and eye rolling.

"Aw, come on," argued Sakura, stifling giggles. "I'm sure they do an *egg*cellent job."

"The plan will go *over easy*," Naomi agreed.

"That's enough," said Obaachan sternly. She paused the hoversled, craning around to serve them each a piercing glare. "This is nothing to *yolk* about."

HOW TO HIDE A MESSAGE IN A RAW EGG
Instructions by Cordelia,
the Anduvia village apothecary
as recorded by Zed

- Get a raw chicken's egg.

- Soak it in vinegar for 4-6 hours. This makes the shell softer.

- Carefully cut a tiny slit in the top of the shell with a sharp, thin knife. The shell should slice instead of cracking.

- Write your message on a small slip of paper and stick it through the slit. (Need to use a waterproof ink? Or maybe cover the paper in wax. It's going to be sitting in wet egg goop.)

- Soak the egg in cold water until the shell firms back up. The slit should seal itself so the egg doesn't leak.

- Looks like a totally normal egg. Whoever cracks the egg will find the message paper inside.

CHAPTER 9
PLOTTING AND PEELING

Corvus and Orion returned to the base shortly after Obaachan's crew. Then there was another meeting to discuss whatever Obaachan had learned. But since they didn't understand the code, the kids could only speculate about the new developments. And as usual, they were *not* invited to this meeting. Once again, they were banished upstairs with Fatima and Orion. But this time, no one felt much like playing games.

"It's not fair," Dominic grumbled. "I get kicked out of all the meetings for being too young, but the first time there's actually something to *do*, suddenly I'm too old!"

"Tell me about it," said Celia. "Everyone else got to go on a secret mission, and we got stuck chopping vegetables and scrubbing crusty porridge out of mugs."

"*I'm* not too old," Linus pouted, "and I *still* got left out!"

"The leaders are just doing what they think is best," said Fatima, but Zed could tell her heart wasn't in it. She probably wished they'd invited her to the meeting too. "They're trying to keep you out of danger."

"Out of danger?" Celia scoffed. "In case you hadn't noticed, we are *all* in danger. The base was supposed to be this unbeatable secret fortress keeping us all hidden, but it *failed*. We have no idea who broke in, or how, or whether anyone else made it out, or whether our families are okay. If a massive base covered by an entire mountain can't keep the bad guys out, how are we supposed to be safe in a busted old shack?"

Usually, Tuesday was in the habit of taking the opposite side of whatever Celia thought, purely on principle. But this time, she had to admit her nemesis had a point. The adults might think that keeping them in the dark about the details would stop them from worrying, but they were in the same amount of danger either way. And it wasn't working, anyway. They weren't just worried. They were *mad*.

Orion slumped back against the wall and scowled. "I'm not putting up with it anymore. If they're not going to treat me like a real agent, then maybe it's time to take matters into my own hands. Sitting around talking is getting us nowhere. It's time to *do* something!"

Dominic was all over that idea. "What did you have in mind?" he asked eagerly.

"I'm scheduled for the first watch duty tonight," said

Orion. "It's only a quarter league to Anduvia. Let's go on a mission of our own. The second guard shift won't start for hours. We'll be back before anyone even knows we were missing."

"Won't someone else be on duty with you?" Fatima pointed out. "*They'll* know. And you can't just leave, anyway! Who will guard the safe house?"

"Great idea," said Orion. "I'll switch the schedule around so we're assigned the same shift. You can stay on watch while the rest of us sneak out. No one will ever know the difference."

Fatima didn't argue. She just bit the inside of her cheek and stared out the window.

"What's this plan, anyway?" Linus asked.

"If the whole problem is that no one pays attention to us, I figure—why not use that to our advantage? Obaachan was right. I watched you in the village today, and you were practically invisible. It wasn't just sliding through the crowd easily, either—even the vendors in the market ignored you. They assumed children wouldn't have any money, so they looked right past you. Let's use this invisible superpower to leave a message they *won't* be able to ignore."

"Message?" Fariq asked. "But Obaachan already sent messages to all the Resistance allies. Who else are you trying to talk to?"

A rebellious grin washed over Orion's face. *"Everyone."*

———

Sitting on a secret, even someone else's secret, felt to Zed like trying to hide a beehive in his chest. His nerves were buzzing with guilty anxiety. He decided to stay as busy as possible to prevent giving Orion's plan away. Which worked out perfectly, because as soon as the meeting was over, Solomon called everyone down to prepare for that evening's festivities. After all, they had another seven days of Hanukkah celebrations to keep them distracted from the cloud of uncertainty hanging over the safe house, and now they had Obaachan's entire shopping spree to choose from. No more making do with goopy cheese rolled in crumbled up biscuits—tonight they could have a proper Hanukkah spread.

At first, Tuesday and Zed got put on rutabaga duty with Professor Orpin. But when Obaachan saw the way Orpin hacked at the leathery vegetable skins, she snatched the peeler right out of his hands and shooed him off to set the table instead. "My Argo was always rubbish with vegetables too," she said, settling herself on a stack of empty crates in front of the sink. "When he married Mavra, I warned her she was going to have to put up with substandard kitchen help, but she didn't seem to mind." She chuckled. "He was such a handsome young man, and I'm sure that spiffy Royal Guard uniform didn't hurt either. Besides, she had such a talent for tending to growing things—flowers, or fritters, she was good enough with plants for the both of them."

"Who are you talking about?" Tuesday asked.

"Why, your grandparents, of course! My son Argo and—well, I suppose most everyone calls her the General now, but I never got on board with all that puffery. 'Don't forget where you came from,' I always say."

"I've been trying to figure that out myself," said Zed. "What to call the General, I mean. I spent my whole life missing out on having grandparents, and now that I finally have one, she doesn't seem very interested in the job."

Obaachan didn't take her eyes from her work. "Have you asked her what she'd like to be called?"

"Not exactly. I hadn't worked up to that part yet. Back at the base, I tried a few times to invite her to eat dinner with our family somewhere quieter than the dining hall or help me and Mom work on a puzzle we checked out of the base library. But she's always too busy. I know she's got a lot of people counting on her, but I'm starting to wonder if it's more than that." Zed sighed and set down his vegetable peeler. "Maybe she doesn't like Tuesday and me."

Obaachan abandoned her half-peeled rutabaga and pulled both kids into a side hug, slimy hands and all. "Oh, my darling pigeons… Mavra's heart was so broken when she thought her boys were gone. She had to put on a lot of armor just to keep going—not literally, you understand, not to shield her body—but she's spent so many years guarding her feelings that she's forgotten how to take that armor off again. Of course she's overjoyed to have her son back, and a new daughter and grandchildren to boot. But

I think having her deepest wish come true might seem too good to be real. And she's never had to be a grandmother before, so she doesn't really know how. She's… afraid."

"Afraid?" Tuesday repeated doubtfully. "Of us?"

"Afraid to be tender after so many years of being tough," Obaachan explained. "Afraid it could all be taken away from her again."

"Maybe she'd feel better if she could ease into the change," Tuesday suggested. "Couldn't you teach her how to do grandma stuff? I mean, you've had the job a long time." She glanced over the woman's wrinkled face and suppressed a grin. "A really, *really* long time."

Obaachan's eyes twinkled with mischief as she aimed a playful splash in Tuesday's direction. "I'll start a grandma boot camp the moment we get this mess at the base sorted out. If she's going to learn, she might as well learn from the best!"

Zed beamed. "That sounds great! I still don't know what to call her, though…"

"Well, she can't have 'Obaachan'," the old woman answered. "That one's taken."

CHAPTER 10
HANUKKAH,
TAKE TWO

They peeled and sliced their way through the mountain of rutabagas until only a sink full of ivory chunks remained. While they worked, Obaachan kept them entertained with stories of growing up in Kyoto, back before they had crystal balls and holograms and hoversleds. At their age, she explained, she spent every Diligence season with her grandfather and aunts diving for pearls in Kyoto Bay. Mostly they harvested the oyster meat to sell in the village market, but roughly one oyster in every thousand had a gleaming pearl hiding inside its shell. Her grandfather had a special box he used to store the pearls until they had a large enough batch to sell to the jeweler in Persepolis. "A strange box," she said, "carved of ironwood, which had no lid or hinges. The only opening was a small metal door set in one side, but the door had no lock or key. Grandfather could open it with a touch of his finger, but it would not open for anyone else."

"Years later, when my grandfather died, my mother and aunts went to clean out his house and found the box hidden in his closet. They couldn't open it, so they considered prying the door off with a chisel, but they didn't know what was inside and were afraid they might break whatever it was. At his funeral, my mother mentioned the dilemma to his brother, and he offered to get it open for her. It wasn't quick or clean—it took nearly twenty minutes, and the lock was too misshapen afterwards to close the safe up again—but Uncle Hiroshi's resonance was similar enough to Grandfather's to get the job done."

"Resonance?" Zed asked.

"Everything in nature vibrates at a different speed," Obaachan explained, "even living things. These vibrations are too small for us to see or hear. But they're the reason things have different colors, and why they sound the way they do when something hits them."

"I've heard some opera singers can sing just the right note to shatter a glass," said Tuesday. "That has something to do with vibrations, right?"

"Exactly," said Obaachan. "That's the power of resonance. The door of Grandfather's safe was made from slipsteel, which can be calibrated to match the vibration pattern of its owner. It works best for that person, but a close relative, someone with a similar resonance, could control it in a less precise fashion."

"Your grandpa's safe sounds a lot like those shape-shifting swords the Legion carries around," Zed observed.

"The Royal Guard used them first," said Obaachan. "The Legion didn't exist before Tyrren took over, remember. But yes, the swords are also made from slipsteel. You can imagine how useful that would be—a weapon that can never be turned against its owner, because only the person it was made for can change its resting state. I'll never forget when my Argo first held the sword the Royal Guard commissioned for him. He said it was like he'd been missing a piece of himself his entire life but hadn't known it until he held that sword and finally felt whole—like it was an extension of his own arm. And years later, your father's commissioning ceremony was just the same. Argo had been promoted to Captain by the time Beren finished his apprenticeship, so he got to present Beren with his sword personally. I'd never seen either of them more proud."

"But Dad's sword isn't like the Legion's at all," Tuesday argued. "Theirs look like silver rods when they're not using them. But Dad's is an umbrella."

Obaachan shrugged. "So he changed its resting state to blend in better when he went into hiding. Just like Uncle Hiroshi changing the shape of the door. It takes longer than changing the active state—shifting a simple rod into a sword or an axe or a hammer—but with enough effort and concentration, it can be done." She jerked her head toward the hammock tree. "Go get it, and we'll try it out."

Tuesday and Zed exchanged a startled look. "Get what?" Tuesday asked, painting on her Innocent And Clueless face.

"Don't play coy," Obaachan laughed. "I know you've got the umbrella. I may not see as well as I used to, but I *notice* things just fine. Like the way you try to tuck it out of sight when you climb in and out of that hammock, checking over your shoulder to make sure no one's looking. You might as well toot a flugelhorn and belt out a few verses of the 'Hello, I'm Suspicious' song."

Tuesday's eyes lit up, a wicked delight creeping over her face. "There's a *song*?"

Zed ignored her. He scrambled up the ladder and retrieved the umbrella for Obaachan to examine. She didn't ask why he had his father's weapon, or what he planned to do with it (which was lucky, since Zed didn't know the answers himself.) She just wiped the rutabaga slime off her hands with her apron and held the umbrella up for a closer look.

"What a marvelous disguise!" she declared, examining the umbrella from all angles. "He even changed the color. But from what I hear, a few soldiers have seen it in this form already, so they might be on the lookout for it. Let's see if we can't make it a bit less noticeable—keep it safe for your father until you can return it to him."

Obaachan handed the umbrella back. "Concentrate," she instructed. "Focus on the thing you want it to become."

Zed searched the corners of his imagination but came up empty. What *did* he want it to be? Smaller would be good, obviously, but beyond that his mind was blank.

Obaachan must have sensed his hesitation. "How about a bracer?" She suggested.

"A what?"

"An arm guard," she explained. "If it's wrapped around your arm, no one can steal it from you."

"Unless they cut your arm off," Tuesday pointed out cheerfully.

Again, Zed ignored her. Obaachan held the umbrella against his forearm and pressed his palm over the smooth folds, placing her knobbly hand on top of his. Zed tried to picture the wrist shields he'd seen archers wear in old movies. The details were pretty foggy, but he quickly decided that didn't matter anyway. After all, the whole point was to prevent it from being removed—it didn't need latches or buckles. He squeezed his eyes shut and tried to focus on the shape.

Zed stole a peek.

No change.

Eyes open this time, he tried again. This time, instead of picturing the finished bracer, he tried to focus on the process. He imagined the umbrella melting into a gloopy silver blob, then slithering around his arm and hardening in place.

Slowly, slowly, the umbrella started to soften. The ends

drooped, then shrank toward the center. Zed watched in amazement as the dark color drained away, replaced by a dull metallic finish. Minutes crept by, with the slipsteel becoming less umbrella-shaped every second. When it finally condensed into a globby brick, it started to curl around his arm, the edges inching together until they met on the other side and melded. It wasn't turning out exactly as Zed had pictured, but keeping the transformation going was like trying to hold his breath underwater. This would have to be good enough.

Obaachan pulled her hand away, and they appraised the results. The bracer's surface was covered with soft, swooping ridges where the umbrella's folds hadn't entirely smoothed out, but this came out looking almost intentional—like a decorative touch, rather than an oversight. It fit snugly around his arm, but not tight enough to be uncomfortable. Zed allowed himself a satisfied smile. It worked! He couldn't say the process felt as natural as Obaachan had described, but perhaps that was to be expected—after all, his resonance wasn't a perfect match.

"Good work!" said Obaachan, patting him on the back. "I knew you could do it."

"Cute bracelet," Tuesday teased.

Zed was really giving his sister-ignoring muscles a workout today. He pretended he hadn't heard her and turned back to Obaachan. "Why doesn't the Resistance use slipsteel?" he asked. The long, curved knives Corvus and the other Operations agents tucked into their belts were certainly impressive, but a weapon that could adapt itself to every situation would undoubtedly come in handy. (Plus, shapeshifting swords were just *cool*.)

Obaachan laughed. "You ducklings think emeralds should fall from the sky! Slipsteel is incredibly rare and expensive, and the expertise to tune its resonance even more so. The last master steelsmith worked exclusively for the royal household, and hasn't been heard from since the coup. We think Tyrren must have coerced her apprentice into making swords for the Legion. And whoever that is, they're assumed to be the only steelsmith left."

Zed started off to haul the rutabaga peelings to the compost bin but turned back as a thought struck him. "Obaachan? Your grandpa's safe—when his brother got it open, what was inside?"

Tuesday rolled her eyes. "Weren't you listening? He kept pearls in it."

But Obaachan shook her head. "Grandfather always sold all the pearls at the end of each diving season. We would have assumed it was empty, except we could hear something shifting around inside when we shook it." A wistful smile stole over her face. "When Uncle Hiroshi opened the safe, we found the strangest thing inside: a single piece of red paper, folded into an origami crane."

"Is that… valuable?" Tuesday asked doubtfully.

Obaachan shrugged. "It was to him."

That night, Captain Solomon added a new candle to the menorah. Tuesday thought it would have been easier to use the same match to light all the candles, but once again, Solomon's routine was deliberate: he used a match to light the center candle, then carried that candle over to light the two off to the side. She supposed this must be important, or he wouldn't bother—but she didn't want to interrupt the ritual by bringing it up. She resolved to ask Levi or Naomi about it later.

Since they took care of the storytelling the night before, today's celebration was devoted to games. They cleared the table away, returning the benches to their stations along the wall and using the cushions as safe bases in a game of Freeze Tag. Then Obaachan taught them how to play Hana Ichi Monme, a game from her childhood no one else had even heard of. It turned out to be something like a cross between Fox, Hunter, Sparrow and Red Rover. All the adults joined in, except for Corvus, who called out advice and encouragement from the sidelines as he set to work knitting a pair of yellow mittens. Fiona helped by pecking at the flashing knitting needles and sneaking off with his extra yarn.

Between games, everyone grazed on the spectacular array of snacks. Tonight's spread still featured apples and nuts and cheeses, but thanks to Obaachan's ingredients there were plenty of new offerings, too. The caramel toffees were a hit, as was the basket of fresh, juicy mangos. Solomon had converted all the rutabaga chunks into a smooth mash, liberally sugared and seasoned with nutmeg and cardamom, which he'd rolled in flour and plopped into a deep pot of boiling oil to make rutabaga puffs. The crisp, crackling outer shell hid a pillowy soft interior. Tuesday decided biting into the warm balls of fragrant sweetness more than made up for the hours of rutabaga wrangling it took to make them.

"Fried foods are a Hanukkah tradition," Levi explained as he sat next to Zed and Tuesday, munching an apple cheese fritter and watching a hilarious adults-only round of Freeze Tag. "To remind us of the oil for the temple's lamp."

They'd been laughing and munching for hours when Corvus consulted his pocket sphere and announced it was time for bed. The party had gone on so long that Zed was certain it must be nearly midnight, but no—according to Corvus it was barely past eight. "The sun sets so early during Providence," he explained. "But the Solstice is only a few days away. After that we'll start getting more daylight."

"We'd better turn in early," said Solomon apologetically. "The adults need to rest up for their guard shifts."

At the mention of guard shifts, Zed's heart jolted into his throat as he remembered what else was coming tonight—Orion's secret mission. He wasn't the only one, either. All around the room, kids were exchanging knowing looks and breaking into whispering clusters.

"But I'm not sleepy!" Linus recited, right on cue. He tried to wink at Orion, but he couldn't figure out how to close only one eye at a time, so it just looked like he was blinking extra hard.

"Me either," Oona agreed. "And it's boring up in the hammock tree. Let's *do* something."

"You have any ideas, Professor?" asked Miel as she collapsed into her hammock.

"Me?" he protested. "But I need to get up for guard duty at four o'clock! I can't stay up all night looking after them."

"I guess I could take them upstairs with me for a bit," Orion suggested casually. "They seemed to like hanging out with me and Fatima earlier. I can keep a lookout while Fatima keeps them busy."

"Nothing too noisy," Solomon warned. "Play a nice, quiet game."

"Oh, don't worry," said Orion, smiling secretly to himself. "You won't even know we're here."

CHAPTER 11
ORION'S MISSION

Zed's breath billowed through the crisp, still night air like a dragon breathing smoke. Come to think of it—more like a Gabriel Hound breathing smoke. He'd be feeling a lot more confident about this mission if he were sitting next to Nyx right now. She'd make the perfect camouflage, a warm, dark shadow disappearing into the night, ready to put both fangs and flames to his defense should anyone so much as look at him wrong. Instead, he was crouched on an icy cobblestone street behind a smelly garbage dumpster with a bunch of equally powerless kids, waiting for Orion to return and give them the all-clear. He pulled his hood lower over his forehead and traced his fingers along the contours of his new bracer. Despite the chill, the slick metal surface gave off a faint warmth, like it was a living thing encasing his arm instead of a disguised contraband weapon. The nearly full moon overhead shone bright enough to make the brick shop fronts and alleys cast shadows.

So far, the plan was going off without a hitch. Fatima

still hadn't seemed thrilled about letting them go, but Orion had managed to convince her it was for a good cause (and that no one else would even know about it). The meadow path and the village streets were both deserted. Now they just needed some supplies.

Just when Zed was sure his toes had gone completely numb, Orion returned. He emerged from the shadows of the nearest alley toting a canvas sack over one shoulder like a ninja Santa Claus, followed by a second cloaked figure carrying an armload of long poles and rolled up poster board. And something about Santa's Little Helper seemed… *familiar.*

The pair approached the dumpster to wave the kids out from their hiding spot. When a beam of moonlight caught the second man's face, Tuesday grimaced.

"*Scrimbley?*" Tuesday spat at Orion, wrinkling her nose in disgust. "What's *he* doing here? You almost ruined everything this morning with your sticky fingers," she added, turning her venom on the smuggler.

"And I feel right terrible about that," said Scrimbley (with questionable sincerity). "Which is why I agreed to make it up to you." He opened the sack and started handing out the contents: a bunch of metal canteens topped with spray heads, and what looked like sheets of black paper. "Orion and I have reached an agreement, you might say. Mutually beneficial. I locate a few supplies for him, and neither of us goes gabbing to the village patrol about the other."

"How are we supposed to help the Resistance with these?" Sakura asked, holding up one of the black sheets.

"It's glue," said Scrimbley. "Stick the sheet where you want it to go, wet it with the spray bottle, and press the poster over top. Simple."

"I get *how* it works," said Dominic, testing out the spray bottle on the dumpster. "You forgot to cover the *why.*"

"Tyrren's got teams posting propaganda in every village," Orion explained. "Figures if people see reminders everywhere that he's in charge, they'll assume everyone else agrees with that and be too scared to argue. We're going to replace them with some advertising of our own. I think it's about time we reminded them who's *really* supposed to be in charge around here."

"Who, the General?" asked Naomi.

"Nope." Orion unfurled a rolled-up poster. "We've got an even better mascot."

Zed stared. In a patch of moonlight, he could just barely make out the portrait of a woman with a long, straight nose and loose brown curls, dressed in a simple white robe. She was guarded by two ravens with piercing red eyes, one perched on each of her shoulders. A golden crown floated symbolically above her head.

"Is that... my mom?" Tuesday asked.

Orion nodded. "The Resistance leadership was already talking about how to let people know Princess Theadora was back. Rumors have been swirling for years that some of the royal family might have survived. But the attack on the base has sped up the timeline—we need to get the word out *now*. Once the villagers realize Tyrren's not their only option, they might get brave enough to stand up to him."

"And the Resistance leaders approved this plan?" Celia asked, grabbing one of the posters for a closer look.

"Well, seeing as most of them are trapped in the base, we can't exactly ask permission, now can we? But I'm sure if the General was here, she'd be all for it."

"Captain Solomon's not trapped," Fariq pointed out. "Did you ask him?"

But Orion wasn't listening. He wove through the clustered kids, passing out more posters.

"Are you sure about this?" asked Oona. "I'm pretty sure messing with other people's walls and windows and stuff is…" she gulped, then whispered the last word: "illegal."

Levi shrugged. "So is joining the Resistance. The people in charge can make laws against anything they want. That doesn't change whether it's right or wrong."

"Look," Orion assured them, "it's not like we're smashing windows or painting over storefronts. We're not hurting anything—just updating the advertising that's already here. And honestly, anything that covers up Tyrren's smug face is doing people a *favor*."

Zed was still staring at the poster. It wasn't a realistic portrait—more like the pictures of kings and queens on playing cards. But despite the regal pose and crown and all, it did actually look quite a lot like his mom. Like it was drawn by someone who had actually seen her. Even though she'd been hiding in an underground base since she returned to Falinnheim…

"Wait a minute," he said, turning to Scrimbley as his brain soaked up the realization. "You knew who my mom *really* was this whole time, didn't you?"

Scrimbley winked at him and tapped his nose. "People always thinks ol' Scrimbley's slow on the uptake, but I makes my living noticing what everyone else is too busy to see. It's me what helped her leave you all those poemy clues, you know."

"Why?" Tuesday asked. "I thought you didn't care about the Resistance. Why are you helping us advertise the Princess being back? In fact—why were you helping my parents in the first place?"

For the first time, Scrimbley actually looked embarrassed. He hadn't blinked at getting caught stealing, but now his gaze turned decidedly shifty. "Don't care one way or the other," he said defensively. "They paid me, is all. I may take on jobs other folk think they're too good for, but I do have one principle: rule number one is 'look out for Number One!'" He jabbed his thumb toward his chest.

Scrimbley quickly changed the subject by pointing out a cobbler's shop he knew had a propaganda poster in the front window. Zed and Tuesday followed him to the brick storefront, which faced directly into the market square.

They must have passed right by it on their errands that morning, but they'd been too busy with the noise and activity of the crowd to notice the poster. Now, in the eerie stillness of the abandoned square, it might as well have had a spotlight trained on it.

Tuesday stared at the poster with a sort of repulsed fascination. She'd been hearing about Tyrren's laundry list of crimes for months now, but he was always referenced at the base as a kind of vague, faceless boogeyman, almost like an anti-mascot. He was a convenient embodiment of everything the Resistance stood against. No matter how different their backgrounds, skills, or goals, the inhabitants of the base could at least agree on one thing: *everyone* hated Tyrren. But this was the first time Tuesday had ever really stopped to think about him as a person. Her eyes raked over the illustrated face, taking in the pale, deep set eyes beneath bushy black brows, the square nose, the silver strands overtaking his dark hair and closely trimmed beard. The man on the poster looked neither sauve and elegantly devious, nor grotesque and horrible. He didn't even have a fancy mustache to twirl while cackling to himself and stroking an equally villainous-looking pet. He was just... normal. Like someone she'd sit across from in the dining hall without a second glance. Not at all the kind of monster she had imagined.

She turned to mention this to Scrimbley, but when she looked up, no one was there but Zed. Scrimbley had slunk away right under their noses.

CHAPTER 12
A HIGH-STAKES ROUND OF MUSICAL SHADOWS

Orion split everyone into groups of four, and they spread out across the deserted cobblestone streets. Every time they found a poster or mural praising Tyrren, one of them covered it with sheets of dehydrated glue and spritzed on some water while the others stretched out a princess poster and patted it into place. The larger murals went higher up the walls than any of them could reach, but Orion passed out poles fitted with a rubber blade at one end that helped them stretch up and squeegee the poster flat.

Tuesday and Zed were working with Lydia and Celia. After covering the mural behind a pawn shop, they stepped back to admire their work. BELIEVE, the walls shouted. THE LIBERATOR, they proclaimed. But now in place of a murderous dictator, those headlines heralded a woman in white, flanked by ravens.

"I get the floating crown bit," Tuesday said, standing back to appraise their work. "But what are the ravens all about? If the artist wanted to show Mom with pets, why didn't they just include Nyx? Gabriel Hounds are more intimidating than birds anyway."

Celia squinted at her with confusion. "Wait, do you really not know?"

"Know what?" Zed asked.

"A pair of ravens is the official symbol of the royal family," Lydia explained. "It was on the seal of the old Regents Council and everything. Doesn't your mom have one?"

"Have what, a raven?"

Lydia shook her head. "No, a royal seal. My parents said that's the only way they believed she really was the missing princess—because she had a ring with the seal on it. They said if an imposter tried to wear the ring, the seal wouldn't show up. Like, it would turn into a flat surface instead."

"An imposter could make a copy of the ring that *wouldn't* go blank," Celia pointed out. "It wouldn't even be hard. They wouldn't need to find slipsteel to make it from—just make a regular ring that always looked the same."

Tuesday glared at her. "Are you calling my mom a liar?"

Zed decided to change the subject before things got out of hand. "Lydia, how do you know so much about this, anyway? There hasn't been a Regents Council since before any of us were born."

Lydia shrugged. "Old library book. I did a history report on the Regents Council a couple years ago, back in Professor Nigume's class."

Zed made a mental note to ask the base librarian about this book, but then he remembered—Lucian, the librarian, was probably hunkered down in the library right now, hiding from the intruders. At least, he hoped so… imagining any alternative scenarios made his stomach churn.

To take his mind off of troubles at the base he latched on to the other interesting tidbit from the conversation—his mother's ring. Zed had seen it for the first time on the day his family was reunited in Falinnheim, when the General had recognized Mom as long-lost royalty. She'd worn it every day since, but he'd never really thought to ask her about it. Now that he thought about it, the engraving of two entwined birds, facing in opposite directions, certainly did look like ravens. He'd never seen the image disappear, but if Celia and Lydia were right, that would only happen if someone *else* tried to wear it. That definitely sounded like slipsteel.

When they finished covering all the propaganda on the block, they had two posters left over, but had run out of glue sheets, so they set off to ask Orion for more. They wound through the maze of alleys, sneaking from shadow to shadow. It was almost like the Musical Shadows game Fatima introduced yesterday, except this time, silence was essential. Also, the stakes were higher; getting caught at this game would lead to a lot more trouble than having to take a turn as "it."

At last they made it back to the deserted market square. Orion was there, all right. But he wasn't standing guard, or putting up posters, or even looking for places to put them. He seemed to be reading the village notice board.

"Good idea," Tuesday said when they reached him. "We should add a poster here too."

Orion didn't respond. Still staring, he tore off one of the papers tacked to the board.

Tuesday peered over his elbow for a better look. It was a missing persons flyer. Tuesday had noticed lots of them on her first trip through Falinnheim, back when she and Zed were collecting nursery rhyme clues. It wasn't unusual, Fatima had explained later, for people to suddenly go missing. Especially if they'd made a habit of annoying Tyrren. But this one was a bit different than all the flyers she'd glanced disinterestedly over before, because this time, she recognized the face beneath the headline. The inked illustration looked a little younger, the jaw a bit softer, the shaggy blonde hair a bit shorter. But it was unmistakably Orion.

Zed and Lydia gathered around to read it too. "*Please help me find my son,*" the ad pleaded. "*Last seen at age 18. Would now be 21. Any leads appreciated—report to Velda the Resolute, 164 East Market Street, West Thebes.*"

"Why does your mother think you're missing?" Tuesday asked.

Orion still couldn't tear his eyes from the paper. He had to clear his throat several times before he answered. "I didn't tell her I was joining the Resistance. Didn't want her to worry. Or try to stop me, I guess. I told her I was switching apprenticeships to work with an ironsmith in a distant coastal town. I thought about sending her a letter or something afterwards, but decided it was too risky. If it got intercepted, the Red Hand might target her just for being related to a Resistance agent. So she has no idea what happened, or if I'm even still alive."

A massive, scarred hand clamped down on Orion's shoulder. "And if you care about her safety," said a low, gravelly voice, "that's the way things will stay."

Everyone jumped. No one had heard Corvus come up behind them—alone, this time. Fiona must have gone to roost for the night. Without a word, he took the flyer from Orion, crumpled it up, and dropped it in his cloak pocket. "Maybe your Ma's looking for you," he added, glancing over the other notices on the board. "But if you went to see her, you can bet the Red Hand would be paying her a visit next. Or could be those scheming weasels posted this ad in the first place, *pretending* to be her. If anyone reported they'd spotted you, their spies could follow your trail back to the rest of the Resistance. Smart plan, really. I'd be impressed, if it wasn't so sinister."

Orion gaped at him. "How did you get here?"

"Walked, same as you. But if you mean *why* am I here, it's

because not all young people's skulls are as thick as yours."

"Fatima," Orion realized with a scowl. "She told?"

Corvus nodded. "And if you'd explained things to the captain half as convincingly as she did, you might have gotten even more help with this half-baked scheme of yours."

Orion gave his boots a sullen inspection. "The captain would never have agreed to it. Then I'd be disobeying a direct order if I went ahead. I figured it would be easier to make it up to him later if I got caught than tip him off before I even got started."

"Apparently that line of thinking gets you in all kinds of trouble," said Corvus. "Your Ma and I should have a good gossip about it over tea sometime."

If leaving the safe house without permission didn't count as insubordination, Zed thought, then arguing with his lieutenant certainly did. But apparently Orion didn't care anymore. Besides outranking him, Corvus was also an entire head taller than the young agent, and several decades older, and could easily be mistaken for the kind of brutish ogre urban legends were made of. But that didn't stop Orion from squaring up to the man's chest and scowling into his battle-scarred face.

"I gave up *everything* to join the Resistance," he spat. "My home, my family, my friends, all my plans for the future—I left it all behind because standing up to Tyrren was more important. I put up with the cat-and-mouse games, went along with the captain's slow and steady strategy. But now the enemy's gotten bold enough to attack us directly, and you expect me to sit around and *wait?* Wait for *what?* I didn't sacrifice everything I cared about so I could lounge around twiddling my thumbs, hoping for reinforcements that are never coming."

Orion was really building up steam now, and Corvus didn't interrupt him. "Tyrren wants to keep everything calm," he went on, "just make his problems disappear, pretend everyone's on board with his plans. And so far, he's been getting away with it. Well I figure, if Tyrren's going to win anyway, we might as well let people know who we are before he has us all killed. I don't care if the captain approves. I don't even care if it *works*. I may not be able to take on the entire Legion alone, but I am *not* going down quietly!"

Zed braced himself for Corvus to shout back, or maybe even punch Orion. For a moment, the icy streets echoed with silent tension as the two men stared each other down. And then, incredibly, Corvus reached forward and pulled the seething young man into a hug. "I know, lad," Corvus murmured. "I gave it all up, too. We all did."

At first Orion attempted to struggle out of his grip, but he soon relented. He'd have better luck escaping a grizzly bear's clutches. Corvus held on so long the situation sailed right on past Awkward and ventured well into Boredom territory.

Calmer now, Orion cleared his throat. "So I guess you're

going to order us back to the safe house?"

"Yep," said Corvus, finally releasing Orion and taking a step back. "You bumbling lot of miscreants are to report back there immediately." His face split into a crooked grin. "Right after we finish this mission."

Corvus rambled off to find more places they could slap a poster over Tyrren's smug face. Zed and Tuesday joined Orion. Maybe he figured it was time to wrap things up before they got caught a second time, Zed thought. Or maybe he was pleased to learn that, even though Fatima had gone to the captain with his secret, she'd argued in favor of his plan instead of just ratting him out. But whatever Orion was thinking, he seemed to have a new bounce in his step as he whisked them around corners and through alleys, scanning the brick walls for places that could use a little decoration. In no time at all they found a home for every last poster. But just as Corvus was doing a headcount to make sure he'd rounded up all the kids, Orion spotted something. He doubled back toward a bookstore.

"Blast!" he said, frowning at a mural in the neighboring alley. "We missed one."

Tuesday handed him some glue sheets. "Might as well cover it up, even if we don't have a poster to replace it with."

Orion hesitated over the painted bricks. Instead of blotting out Tyrren's face, he went for the writing framing the mural. THE LIBERATOR, it proclaimed. BELIEVE.

He tore one sheet into strips, which he used to black out some of the letters. Then he cobbled the scraps together to make a few new letters, squeezing in additions above and between the painted text.

"There," he said, standing back to survey his work with satisfaction.

Tyrren's portrait now smiled benevolently over a very different message:

THE ■ *t* RA*i* TOR ■ LIE*s* ■

Orion hummed a victorious tune to himself as he strutted back to join Corvus at the market square.

Tuesday and Zed hung back for a moment to admire the new masterpiece. "We should have done that with all the others!" Tuesday laughed.

Zed wasn't quite sure how he felt about this secret mission. Sure, he wanted some way to help the Resistance, but he wasn't entirely convinced graffiti was going to make enough of a difference. He was about to bring this up with Tuesday, but he never got the chance. Because at that moment, a gloved hand clamped down over his mouth, and everything went dark.

CHAPTER 13
THE REAL DEAL

Drip.

Drip.

Drip.

Zed scrunched his eyes closed even tighter. He was on his bedroll, back in his family's quarters at the base. Dad must be up early to get ready for his duty shift. He'd left the faucet dripping after rinsing out one of those foaming dental beads…

But then why had Nyx let him keep sleeping? The moment one family member was awake, she always started slurping faces so the others would get up too.

And then his memory caught up with his ears. He wasn't home at all, or even in his hammock at the safe house. He had been kidnapped. *Again.*

Of course, all the other attempts so far had been a lot less effective. Between the Legion, the Red Hand, and the Resistance, so far only Captain Solomon had actually succeeded in capturing the most wanted kids in Falinnheim.

And since his intervention had actually prevented a completely separate kidnapping attempt by angry, armed soldiers, Zed was willing to let that one slide. But apparently, someone had just broken Solomon's record.

His eyes squinted into focus, but that didn't help much, because the room was nearly as dark with them open as when he was dreaming. He was lying on a rough stone floor, surrounded by a jumble of overturned metal buckets, an array of bristly scrub brushes, and one unconscious sister. The dripping noise continued, but it turned out to belong to a wet mop standing up in the corner to drain. Zed felt around in his cloak pockets with a jolt of panic, then let out an anxious breath; his notebook was still there. If whoever abducted them had taken it, they might have learned about Obaachan's egg messages.

He nudged Tuesday, who sat up with a gasp. She looked around wildly, but then she remembered the alley, and the surprise attack, and blacking out.

"Let me guess," she sighed, slumping back against a bin of dirty linens. "The Red Hand got us?"

"Looks like it," said Zed, adding a sigh of his own. "Unless you know somebody else with those weird numbing gloves."

"Where are we now?"

Zed stood up and tiptoed to the door. He tried the handle—locked, of course. He put his ear to the rough, solid wood, but he couldn't hear anything happening beyond it.

"Some kind of laundry room?" he guessed, looking around at the dim shadows thrown by the clutter of cleaning products. A single crystal embedded above the door frame gave off a faint pink glow, but that was the only source of light. It was difficult to make out much detail.

"Scrimbley!" Tuesday spit out suddenly.

"What?"

"That dirty, cheating lowlife double-crossed us! He acts like this great guy, doing favors for the Resistance, and then runs off and snitches on us while we're too busy to notice. I guess 'looking out for Number One' means turning us over to Tyrren's spies the first chance he gets." She balled up her fists and scowled. "He was probably planning that the moment he agreed to help Orion."

Zed frowned. The eerie Red Hand agents were easy to villainize, slinking along in the shadows, waiting to pounce on anyone that attracted their interest. But they actually *knew* Scrimbley... or at least, they thought they did.

"How would he know where to find the Red Hand in the first place?" Zed pointed out. "They don't exactly make obvious patrols, like the Legion."

"He wasn't shy about threatening to rat us out to the Legion," Tuesday reminded him. "Why not the Red Hand too? I wouldn't put anything past that coward to save his own skin."

"I think he was just saying that to get Orion off his back. Scrimbley doesn't want soldiers *or* the secret police paying attention to him. He's not about to flag them down and risked getting arrested himself."

"The Red Hand doesn't arrest people," Tuesday grumbled. "They make people *disappear*."

SKREEEEEK. Zed and Tuesday scrambled to their feet as the door swung open. A gloomy-looking man in starched black robes bowed to them, then motioned them stiffly into the hall. "Please follow me."

Tuesday's first impulse was to kick him in the shins and make a break for it. But she figured escapes were usually a lot more successful when you started with some idea of where you were. As though he'd read her mind, Zed shook his head slightly, then followed the man into the hall. Now was not the time for heroics.

The crystal sconces spaced along the hallways were still lit, but when they passed by connecting corridors with open foyers, the weak sunshine creeping across the intersections told them morning had arrived. Unlike their last encounter with the Red Hand's unconsciousness gloves, apparently this one had managed to knock them out for the entire night.

After marching through a maze of hallways and up three separate stairways, the butler led them into what appeared to be a massive banquet hall. Their footsteps echoed off gleaming marble floors and gilded, mirrored walls. A polished wood table stretched all the way across the room. There would have been space to seat hundreds of people, except there weren't any chairs or plates or silverware. Just a long, lonely, empty table.

When he noticed them lagging behind, the butler doubled back and nudged them onward. Tuesday fought the temptation to stomp on his foot and settled for an insolent scowl instead. She kept on marching along the deserted table, but halfway there, she realized it was not empty after all. A gentle clinking noise wafted over from the far end of the room. At the head of the table, a single person sat under the sparkling chandelier, stirring a clear goblet with a silver spoon. The steaming liquid inside started out a vivid shade of purple, but as he stirred it gradually shifted to a deep, rich magenta.

Zed was so busy theorizing how color changing tea might work that he almost forgot about the person stirring it. At first, they were still too far away to pick out many details. But the closer they walked, the more familiar the man became. Those eyebrows, darker than his silver-streaked hair, the cold blue eyes—they'd been studying that face all night. It had been easy to sneer at the Tyrren on murals and posters, but now they were face to face with the real thing.

CHAPTER 14
THE LIBERATOR'S PROPOSAL

Did he know? Playing innocent was usually Tuesday's go-to strategy. Maybe the Red Hand didn't realize they'd just captured the children of Falinnheim's last surviving royalty (not to mention the grandchildren of the Green Fly). And if they didn't realize who they'd captured, Tyrren might not either. Maybe they were just mad about the posters? But, no—the spies always seemed to know *more* than they were willing to reveal, not less. And somehow, she didn't think a little underage vandalism was enough to warrant a meeting with the dictator of an entire dimension.

Tyrren laid down his spoon and looked up from his golden plate. He smiled. "Ah—so glad you could join me for breakfast! Please, take a seat."

He snapped his fingers. Three servants sprang from the wall, sliding ornately carved dining chairs into place on either side of him and setting the table with more of the gleaming dishes. More servants followed, pouring them each a glass of the purple tea and stacking their plates high with pastries and sausages. Finally, a chef in a long white apron ladled on steaming mounds of scrambled eggs.

Tuesday stared. *Eggs!* Had Obaachan's message arrived already? Which of the kitchen staff had intercepted it? Maybe he was toying with them, ordering his lackeys to deliver them to a banquet just so he could watch them squirm over their failure. Her eyes flicked to Tyrren's face, but he'd gone back to calmly stirring his tea. If he intended to confront them with captured evidence, he was certainly playing it cool.

"Please, sit," he repeated, gesturing at the chairs again.

The butler cleared his throat loudly and gave them another nudge.

Zed and Tuesday sat.

"I apologize for my friends' uncivilized behavior," Tyrren said between sips. "I was furious when I learned how rudely they'd treated my guests. There was no surely call for those horrible red gloves of theirs. But I suppose we must allow them a little grace. Their hearts were in the right place, after all. Children, wandering frozen alleys at night with a band of lawless ruffians! Naturally, they had to rescue you."

"Rescue?" said Tuesday coldly. "Is that what they call kidnapping around here? And I doubt any of the Red Hand even *have* hearts."

Tyrren laughed—not a villainous Cartoon Evil Mastermind kind of laugh, but as though Tuesday had just told a joke he found particularly charming. "Oh, they told me you were clever!" he chuckled, waggling a finger at her. "'No hearts'… I'll have to write that one down."

The unexpected cheerfulness threw Tuesday off balance for a second. But only a second. "Do you invite all your 'guests' to sleep locked in the laundry room?" she tried next.

"I'm afraid that was for your own protection. Of course the palace has guest rooms and feather beds aplenty, but I was concerned you might wake up disoriented and get rash ideas about tying bedsheets together and climbing out a window. And it would be such a shame if you were to fall to your deaths before you'd had a chance to hear my proposal."

The ominous phrasing did not escape Zed's notice. *Before.* As though an unfortunate "accident" *after* they'd refused whatever sinister plot he had in mind was still a possibility.

Tyrren snapped his fingers again. The butler scurried over and leaned in while Tyrren whispered something to him, then bowed himself out of the room.

"Please, eat," Tyrren urged, spearing a sausage with his fork. "We're just waiting for two more guests to join us, and then we can get down to business."

Last time they'd been captured, it was Captain Solomon referring to them as "guests" and offering them food. But of course, that was before they understood who Solomon was, or the Resistance for that matter, so they weren't feeling particularly trusting yet. That time, Tuesday erupted with panic when Zed actually dared to eat any—what if it was poisoned or something? But this time, it was Zed who hesitated over his plate. Tyrren was happily munching away, but that didn't prove anything; they hadn't been served at the same time, so he couldn't be sure their food was from the same batch. And they already knew he was a murderer.

Zed looked across the table at Tuesday. She was staring at Tyrren, arms folded, wearing a scowl that could curdle milk. "You haven't given us any forks," she said.

Tyrren smiled to himself and took another sip of tea. "Pity. The kitchen crew probably just got lazy. I find it near impossible to keep competent servants on staff." But there were a dozen servants lined up against the wall behind him, and he made no attempt to correct them.

If this was Tyrren's attempt at forcing social embarrassment, Zed thought, he had seriously underestimated who he was dealing with. His sister tended to take power plays as a challenge. Sure enough, Tuesday locked her glare on Tyrren as she scooped up a glob of the gooey eggs with her bare hands. She slurped it up with her tongue as grossly and noisily as possible. If Tyrren found it funny to embarrass her, she would simply refuse to be ashamed of *anything*.

Zed shrugged and helped himself to a pastry.

The butler returned, followed by a slim man with a

long, dour face, and a young woman carrying an electronic notepad. Tyrren snapped again; servants dashed off the wall with a chair and plate (but no food) for the man and seated him next to Zed. The woman was not offered anything, and remained standing a respectful distance from the table. Then the butler and kitchen staff bowed themselves out of the banquet hall, leaving Tyrren to speak to his "guests" in private.

"Children," Tyrren said, still not looking up from his breakfast, "I'd like you to meet Sylas. He's an old friend of your father's, currently leading my intelligence agency. He's about to explain how it's possible for your parents to be alive. Or for the two of you to *exist*, for that matter. He had assured me, many years ago, that your parents did not survive the tragic attack on the last Moderator's household."

Zed and Tuesday looked at each other, and then at Sylas. Did he mean this was the leader of the Red Hand? And what exactly did he mean by "old friend"?

Sylas said nothing.

"This is astonishing and welcome news, of course," Tyrren added. "How fortunate that Princess Theadora was spared the horrible fate the rest of her family suffered! And as an eyewitness to the event, perhaps she will finally be able to set the record straight on what occurred that tragic day. Although..." He paused, stroking his chin in thought. "Curious, isn't it? Where has the princess been all this time? Why did she not return sooner? And once she returned, why didn't she present herself in the capital immediately to report the truth? It's almost as if she's… *hiding* something."

"Don't play dumb!" Tuesday retorted. "Everyone knows *you* killed all those people and took over the government. How else would you be in charge now?"

"*I?*" Tyrren looked thoroughly scandalized. "I have never killed anyone. In the absence of the Regents Council, I agreed to take on the burden of leading Falinnheim. But the suggestion I had anything to do with their deaths is absurd."

"*You're* absurd!" Tuesday shot back.

(Not her finest work, Zed had to admit. His sister must be getting flustered.)

Tyrren smiled. "Although I had been privileged to serve as an advisor to the Regents Council for many years, I was away on business on the day of the attack, so I can't be sure what happened. Sylas was there, though," he added, as though the thought had just occurred to him. "Perhaps he can enlighten us."

Stone-faced as ever, the man cleared his throat and recited, as though he'd practiced his explanation hundreds of times. "I was serving as First Lieutenant of the Royal Guard. The first shift of the day had just begun. All the guards attended the captain's daily briefing and then dispersed to our stations. I was assigned with three other guards to the council chambers. Everything seemed to be proceeding normally, but then the regents did not arrive for their scheduled council session. I sent a guard to check on them, who found them all dead in their rooms. The guards assigned to each regent were missing. We can only speculate whether the guards were also killed and their bodies removed by the assassins; were captured and then killed elsewhere; or perhaps had a hand in the plot themselves."

"How tragic," Tyrren said, shaking his head mournfully. "And none of the regents' guards were heard from again?"

"The Royal Guard was dissolved after the event and replaced by two separate organizations: one for village patrols, and the other for the Liberator's personal security. As the highest-ranking former guard, I was chosen to lead the security and intelligence-gathering force. Though rumors swirled for years about their fate, we uncovered no trace of the missing guards or regents until two weeks ago, when two of my agents reported an unusual disturbance in Kyoto."

It took all Zed's willpower to keep his face blank. He was pretty sure there were several lies tucked into Sylas's account, but that last one stood out like a blinking neon sign. The fight in Kyoto was *months* ago, not weeks. Sylas *knew* that, and he knew that his captives knew it. Unless the agents involved had delayed their report? Or perhaps that was the timeline Sylas wanted Tyrren to believe…

Sylas continued. "Two people strongly resembling the missing Princess Theadora and her guard Beren the Vigilant engaged in an altercation with two soldiers, in the company of a Gabriel Hound and two children. The agents attempted to take them into custody but were prevented by the hound's unnatural powers. They elected to report in and await further evidence. Last night, the same children were spotted as part of a gang vandalizing walls and shop windows in Anduvia. The agents overheard the children describe an illustration of Princess Theadora as depicting their mother."

Zed had another idea: maybe Sylas was sprinkling a few errors into his account on purpose, hoping one of them would jump in and correct him. Then they'd be admitting to all the rest of it. He glanced over at Tuesday, hoping she wasn't about to take the bait. But Tuesday was far too busy making a show of dunking a pastry into her tea, allowing the sopping lump to drip all over the table before she took a bite. Zed was pretty sure she was actually listening to Sylas's account, but so far she hadn't given anything away. And in the meantime, evidently she intended to make her contempt for the proceedings crystal clear.

"How fortunate your agents were able to rescue these poor, misguided children!" Tyrren gushed. He turned to Zed. "I don't blame the two of you for falling in with the wrong crowd, of course. Playing on family loyalties to get you to do their dirty work for them—it's really quite insidious. A few rebels and malcontents want to stir up trouble, so they collect confused refugee children and convince them they'd be *important,* if only their mother was in charge. But when the plan failed, did they stick their necks out to defend you? No—the cowards let children take the blame."

Zed bit his tongue. Orion wasn't using them! He understood how it felt to be overlooked, and had offered them a chance to do something about it. It wasn't his fault they'd been captured. But an unwelcome thought kept gnawing at the back of his mind. *Invisible*, Obaachan had called them. She talked up all the benefits of acting undetected, like it was some kind of superpower to be ignored. But in a way, she had treated him with the same shortsighted disrespect she mocked the villagers for. She'd made her own plans without even consulting Captain Solomon, and treated all the kids she could get her hands on as props to avoid suspicion. No one *asked* if they wanted to be involved in any of this. Obaachan, Solomon, Orion, even his parents— they all carried on with their own priorities and expected the "invisibles" to play along. Obaachan loved him—Zed was sure of it. She hadn't been trying to put him in danger or get him in trouble. But there was just enough truth plastered over Tyrren's lies to make them stick to his brain.

"Of course, everyone knows the rebels are nothing but lowly criminals," said Tyrren. "The real question is, why would the last regent want to be involved with such scum? After all, we don't know who organized the attack. It could have been the same vandals trying to slander the government last night. Unless…" Tyrren dropped his fork and allowed it to clatter dramatically to his plate. He gasped, as though he'd just been struck by a horrible realization. "Unless Princess Theadora planned the attack herself?"

Tuesday had enough. She leaped to her feet, knocking her chair to the floor as she glared at Tyrren. "You take that back! That's a dirty lie, and you know it!"

"Think about it," he whispered dramatically, ignoring Tuesday's outburst. "The Princess had just been appointed to the Regents Council. But with dozens of senior regents in line ahead of her, she'd have to wait *decades* for her turn to be crowned Moderator. And her guard—wasn't he the captain's son? Also last in line, eager for a chance to make his mark with the Royal Guard. Perhaps they plotted together to get all those inconvenient people out of the way and seize power for themselves. They could pretend they'd been victims too, lucky to escape with their lives, then waltz into the aftermath and take over."

For one horrible moment, Zed didn't know what to think. Tuesday had spent their entire childhood trying to convince him their parents were hiding something. And no matter how he had tried to explain away all their odd, suspicious behavior, in the end Tuesday had been right. Well, not about the specifics—the "on the run from an alternate dimension" explanation had been a bit far-fetched, even for her imagination—but Mom and Dad *had* been keeping dramatic secrets. About Nyx, and the transporting compass, and Scrimbley, and Falinnheim. They'd even lied about their names. To their own children! And even after returning to Falinnheim, they were never willing to discuss what went on in all those secret meetings at the base. Was it so impossible they were still hiding things?

"I'm sorry to have to break the news to you," said Tyrren with a sad, patronizing smile. "You're not to blame. It's only natural for you to take your parents' side. But they lied to you. *They're* the ones you should be angry with, not me."

Zed stole a despairing glance at his sister, silently pleading with her to come up with something—*anything*—to explain it all away. A congealed ball of all his doubt and suspicion, resentment and guilt settled at the bottom of his stomach: a slimy, poisonous mass that threatened to seep into every strand of his brain. He couldn't believe he was giving Tyrren's words a second thought, but every time he tried to push the explanations away, those persistent thoughts slithered right back in. Everything they'd learned about Falinnheim's history had come from people aligned with the Resistance. But what if the entire Resistance was founded on a lie?

"Don't worry," Tyrren soothed. "I'll protect you. You can live in my palace, have servants to attend to your every whim. All I ask is that you help set the record straight."

"Protect us?" Tuesday sneered. "From what?"

Tyrren's forehead creased with concern. "From your parents, naturally. After all, if they were power-hungry enough to wipe out all those people sixteen years ago, they're capable of anything. Anyone who knows what really happened would have to be silenced. I'm afraid you are both in incredible danger."

And just like that, the spell was broken. Zed threw back his head and laughed. He'd almost fallen for it! But Tyrren pushed his story one lie too far, and the entire illusion came crashing down.

"You really thought we'd buy that?" said Zed incredulously. Now that he'd seen through Tyrren's plan, it collapsed under the weight of all those stacked-up fantasies. Waves of calm and confidence washed over him with every word he spoke, the truth wrapping itself around him like a force field. "None of it makes any sense!" he scoffed. "No one would kill for the chance to lead the Regents Council, because the Moderator didn't even get a vote. It would make more sense to want to be a regent as long as possible. And my mom was the youngest member—she had decades of important decision-making to look forward to. Her voice wasn't ignored. In fact, by joining the council, she had just *stopped* being invisible."

"But with everyone else gone, she'd be the *only* voice," said Tyrren quickly. "She could do away with the council entirely."

"So why run?" Tuesday challenged. "If that was the plan all along, being the only survivor would have meant *success*. But she's not the one strutting around, calling herself the Liberator—you are."

"If what you're suggesting was true, you'd have switched

places," Zed realized. "She'd be the dictator taking over, and you'd be in hiding, or trying to stop her. No… the only part of the plan that failed was that my parents survived. It's easy for you to paint the Resistance as criminals when you're the one making all the laws. But now that my parents are back in Falinnheim, you're panicking, because they know what really happened. They know *you* killed all those people."

But none of those reasons mattered, in the end. His parents loved him. That was enough. And anyone who thought they could convince him otherwise was too pathetic to bother arguing with.

Tyrren shrugged. "Oh, well," he said carelessly. "It was worth a shot, at least. But you're still wrong about that last point, you know." He settled back comfortably in his chair and dabbed his mouth with a napkin.

"Oh, yeah?" Tuesday challenged. "Wrong about what?"

"*I* didn't kill all your relatives," Tyrren said smugly, pointing down the table at Sylas. "*He* did."

CHAPTER 15
TRUTH, LOYALTY, AND THE KEYS TO SUCCESS

Tyrren smiled to himself, like he was entertaining party guests with an anecdote that made him look especially clever. "As I said before, I was away on business. I was nowhere near Alexandria on the day of the attack, let alone the palace. I have dozens of eyewitnesses to prove it—I made certain of that. I couldn't allow Falinnheim to be led into a new era by a murderer. No, what I said was true. I have never killed anyone. Sylas and the other guards took care of that."

He snapped his fingers at the woman lingering in the shadows behind his chair. She marched forward and held her tablet at the ready. "Of course, I think the version that discredits your parents makes the more compelling narrative," Tyrren continued, "so we'll be going with that one. Meet my information minister, Eris. She's responsible for making sure all of Falinnheim is thinking and talking about the correct issues."

The young woman's fingers flew across the tablet, logging away Tyrren's orders. "If two children can poke holes in the story, some of the villagers might too," she said without looking up. "Should I put out a few alternate versions as well? Perhaps with Sylas witnessing the attack and attempting to capture the rebel Regent?"

"The Rebel Regent," Tyrren repeated, as though his tongue was taking the words for a test drive. "I like it. Be sure to use that when you turn those silly Resistance posters into 'wanted fugitive' notices." He rubbed his hands together eagerly. "That Green Fly character was getting old anyway. A scheming princess will make a much better villain."

Tuesday was juggling so many new revelations at once, she had a tough time deciding which one to insult first. So she decided to take them down in order. "You really expect us to believe anything you have to say, after the load of hot garbage you tried to pass off already? Why would Sylas do all your dirty work? And why would he keep working for you, if you're so quick to throw him under the bus when you get caught lying?"

Tyrren just peered at her curiously. "What's a bus?"

Tuesday started to argue, but he cut her off with an

impatient wave of his hand. "Never mind, I don't care. The point is, Sylas understands *loyalty*. He was stuck playing second fiddle in the Royal Guard, held back by a selfish captain who didn't properly reward his years of service. I created a foolproof plan to get him the power and respect he deserved. Why wouldn't he want to help carry it out? And now that he's earned his reward, he's happy to do whatever I ask. And besides, you're just *children*. You think the leader of the Red Hand, feared and fabled across the whole of Falinnheim, is worried you might tattle on him? Even if anyone believed you, the story would only make him that much more powerful." He paused thoughtfully, then laughed. "I just now realized—Sylas helped organize the other guards to kill your mother's family. As the Moderator, her grandfather was the major concern, but all the Regents were your aunts and uncles, cousins and grandparents. How silly of me—I nearly forgot about your father's side of the family. The Captain of the Royal Guard wasn't on board with our little plan, so of course he had to go too. That means Sylas here killed *both* your grandfathers!" He turned to Sylas, still laughing. "Didn't you take care of the captain personally? I can't recall his name…"

Sylas's face betrayed no hint of emotion. "Argo," he reminded Tyrren. "Argo the Just."

"That's right. Yes, poor old fool was completely caught off guard. I guess he 'just' didn't see it coming!"

Tuesday was rarely at a loss for words, but no insult or

snappy retort could make a dent in such callous cruelty. Only a few minutes ago, she'd accused the child-snatching Red Hand of being heartless. But anyone who could first plan a murder, then mock his victims for failing to prevent it, must be truly beyond feeling. There was no point wasting her outrage on him.

Tyrren snapped his fingers again, forgetting he'd already dismissed the butler. When no one dashed to his side to jot down orders, a shadow of annoyance flickered across his face. But only for a second.

"I had really hoped you two would see reason," he said with a long-suffering sigh, "but I suppose expecting children to behave rationally is too much to hope for. If you're not going to help discredit my enemies, then I have no further use for you. Sylas—deal with them."

Zed gulped. It didn't take a lot of imagination to guess what "deal with them" meant.

Sylas started to scoot back his chair but paused when Eris cleared her throat. "If I might make a suggestion, Your Excellence?"

Tyrren nodded.

"The Resistance must know the children were taken. They may be plotting a rescue attempt. It could be strategic to keep the children in place for the moment. We may be able to capture the Green Fly, or his agents, if they attempt to infiltrate the palace. Or perhaps we could offer to exchange them for the Rebel Regent's surrender."

"Fine." Tyrren waved her away. "You take care of the arrangements, then. Have the children scanned for holograms—the rebels will want proof we've still got them."

"A brilliant idea," Eris agreed. "Once we have holograms of the children, we can use them in future information campaigns. A live speech would have been preferable, of course, but we can program holograms to say anything we like. Hearing the Regent's own children denounce her will make quite an impact on the villagers."

Eris finished her notes and started briskly down the room. When Zed and Tuesday didn't immediately follow, she paused, frowning. "Come along. I trust you won't need Sylas's help to behave yourselves?"

Zed resisted the urge to look at Sylas, and shot a silent warning across the table instead. *Cool it, Tuesday, just this once,* he thought. He had no idea how they were going to get out of this, but he was certain their odds were better if Sylas didn't get involved. This was no time to put up a fight.

Tuesday understood. She rolled her eyes but scooted back in her chair and followed Zed and Eris.

The moment the banquet hall doors closed behind them, Tuesday began peppering Eris with questions. "How can you keep working for such horrible people? They just admitted killing a bunch of people and overthrowing the government. You can't *really* want to help them do it?"

"It's nothing personal," the woman answered. She was keeping such a quick pace Zed and Tuesday nearly had to jog to catch up with her. "A job's a job. Besides, I was even younger than you are when all that happened. It's got nothing to do with me. Can't go back and change the past."

"But you know the truth!" Tuesday argued. "You're in charge of getting messages to all of Falinnheim. Don't you want to do something *good* with all that power?"

Eris let out a terse laugh. "The truth? The truth is whatever I tell people it is. And besides, I rarely put out a single version of a story anyway. People love to argue—it makes them feel smart. So I give them two opposing viewpoints to choose from. No matter what the issue is, they'll naturally choose a side so they can bicker with their neighbors about the other. They never stop to think *both* options might be wrong." She glanced back at them with a grin, but kept walking. "Take the Green Fly, for example: some people think he's the most evil, dangerous criminal in history. Every time they see a missing person flyer, they claim it as evidence the Green Fly is a serial kidnapper. On the other hand, some say he's a harmless prankster, or nothing but a legend. Pompous old windbags spend every night in their village taverns debating until they turn blue, but I don't care which they believe. It's just a distraction. Keeps people too busy to worry about anything that matters. And busy people are easy to govern. Especially if they're busy feeling superior and self-important."

Tuesday decided to try a different angle. "You must be really good at your job if you can trick people into talking about whatever you want. But you're right—it *is* just a job. The Liberator and the Red Hand might be in charge, but that doesn't mean you owe them anything. Tyrren makes these big speeches about valuing loyalty, but he doesn't offer loyalty to anyone else. You saw how quick he was to blame Sylas when we saw through his lies."

"You said you were only a kid when Tyrren took over," Zed added. "So you can't have been working for him this whole time. I wonder what happened to the information ministers who came before you?"

Tuesday shook her head gravely. "Murderous dictators don't usually offer cushy retirement options. I bet the first time he got annoyed with them he ordered Sylas to 'take care of it.' Tyrren solves problems by making them someone else's problem."

Eris glanced furtively back at them and sped up even more. "Which is why there's no point fighting him. The only way to win is to play along."

They reached the laundry room. Eris took a key ring from the pocket of her robes and fumbled through it searching for the correct one. Her hands were shaking, making the heavy iron keys clank together with a dull, melancholy music. Finally, she found the right key and thrust it into the lock. She lifted the latch, threw the door open, and shoved Tuesday and Zed inside like she couldn't get rid of them fast enough.

Zed stood in the doorway and locked eyes with Eris.

"Tyrren was going to have us killed," he said quietly. "But you stopped him. Thank you."

Eris stared back in silence, then cleared her throat. "I'll send the butler to fetch you when the hologram scanner is calibrated."

"You're not like them," Zed continued. "You don't have to play along."

The door closed in his face.

Tuesday took out her frustration on a stray bar of soap, kicking it across the room. Whatever it collided with in the dark set off a chain reaction of clangs and thuds as more of the stacked clutter fell over.

Zed sighed. "I actually thought she might listen."

"Coward," Tuesday seethed. "She's just as bad as Scrimbley."

"So what's the plan?"

"We escape, obviously. Preferably before the butler comes back. But I guess if all else fails, we could throw things at him when he unlocks the door and then run for it."

Zed didn't like the sound of that. The palace halls were sure to be crawling with servants and guards; they wouldn't make it around the first corner without getting nabbed. But something about Tuesday's plan sparked an idea...

"Remember Dad's rules?" he asked Tuesday.

"Sure," she said, counting them off on her fingers. "'Don't talk to strangers, always know your exits, don't eat yellow snow.' How's that supposed to help us?"

Zed rolled his eyes. "I was thinking of 'everything can be a tool.' We've got all kinds of stuff right here in the room with us—could be something useful."

"Like what?" Tuesday scoffed. "A spare key? These people are evil, not stupid."

"Won't know until we look. Maybe something we could use to knock the door down, or take it apart. Or maybe there's another exit hidden behind all this junk."

They found a bank of industrial-sized laundry ports built into the far wall, seven boxes of detergent powder, various brooms and mops, and a basket of mismatched socks, but no secret doors or misplaced keys. Tuesday thought about rigging up a broom handle as a lever to pry the door off its hinges, but on further inspection realized the hinges and latch faced the hall. The only thing on their side of the door was the keyhole.

The keyhole! Tuesday knelt down and squinted through it. "I've always wanted to do this," she admitted as she peered out at the hall. "People spy through keyholes all the time in cartoons and stuff, but it doesn't work on the modern doors back home."

Zed thought back to the ring of bulky antique keys Eris had used to open the door. Modern keys looked more like tiny, serrated knives, with grooves along the blade cut to match the lock's tumblers precisely. But this door must be as old as the rest of the palace; its locks had to be big enough to admit the wide rectangular bit at the end of its old-fashioned key, which left a gap big enough to look through. Really, the key to this door must be pretty simple compared to the ones he was used to. Simple *enough*, perhaps…

"The hall looks deserted," Tuesday reported.

"Good." Zed tapped her shoulder and she moved aside. "I want to try something."

He laid his hand on the silver bracer clinging to his arm. Changing its resting state had been a struggle, and he wasn't entirely convinced he'd managed that by himself anyway—he suspected Obaachan had contributed more than just moral support. But now that Dad's sword was responding to his resonance, maybe changing the *active* state would go smoother.

I need a key, Zed thought. He tried to picture the one Eris had used to unlock the door.

To his surprise, the silver bracer slid from his arm and materialized in his other hand as a key. Well—almost. The shining slipsteel was now vaguely key-shaped, with a long, narrow stem suspending a looped handle at one end and a notched rectangular bit at the other. But the finish was clumsy and irregular, like it had been molded from mashed potatoes instead of metal. It was also much heavier than any key he'd ever held before, presumably because the bracer's mass was now packed into a smaller mold.

Tuesday eyed it dubiously. "If that actually works, I'm embarrassed for whoever's in charge of palace security."

"You want to escape, or not?" Zed huffed.

Tuesday stepped back to let him try.

The key slid into the lock. So far, so good…

He tried turning it. No resistance! Now, to try lifting the latch.

It didn't budge. Disappointed, Zed removed the key. "The lock mechanism must be *too* open," he sighed. "The key's not detailed enough to catch any of the moving parts."

"Maybe the shape's fine, but it needs to be bigger," Tuesday suggested. "If the key turned without hitting anything in there…" She had to admit she didn't know much (okay, *anything*) about how locks worked—or slipsteel, for that matter—but she wasn't ready to give up yet. Besides, she hadn't taken a crack at changing the umbrella-sword-bracer herself yet. She was certain she'd be a natural at it.

Tuesday squinted through the keyhole again. "Aaaagh!" she yelled, scrambling backwards.

Someone was peering back at her through the keyhole.

CHAPTER 16
TIME TO GO

Thunk! The lock unbolted.

Shhhhf. The key slid out of the lock.

SKREEEEEK. The hinges groaned as the heavy door eased open.

"Time to go," said the man in the doorway.

Tuesday snatched the slipsteel key from Zed. The moment she touched it the key grew to the size of a baseball bat, which she held menacingly over her shoulder, ready to swing if the man tried to grab them.

"Quickly," the man whispered. "Before the butler comes back. If we hurry, we can get a decent head start before they come looking for you."

"What?" was all Tuesday could think to say. She glanced at the massive key hovering over her shoulder and winced. She'd been trying for a sword.

"Who are you?" Zed asked.

"I'm an undercover palace agent," he said, gesturing them frantically into the hall. "We've got to get going. I can explain more on the way."

Tuesday lowered her weapon. When her grip relaxed, it changed back into an arm bracer, even though no one was wearing it at the moment. She passed it back to Zed, who morphed it into a silver blob, then allowed it to harden into place on his forearm.

"Is it just me," Tuesday whispered to her brother, "or does this guy seem ready to belt out a couple verses of 'Hello, I'm Suspicious'?"

Zed shrugged. "You got any better options?"

Tuesday frowned. "Well if he pulls out a flugelhorn, I'm out of here."

Cautiously, she and Zed tiptoed through the doorway. Once their eyes adjusted to the light, they got their first proper look at their rescuer: a short, tanned, curly-haired man wearing a stained linen apron over a plum-colored tunic and trousers.

"How did you know where to find us?" Tuesday asked suspiciously.

The man took off down the hall, forcing them to scurry after him to hear the answer. "I've been working in the palace kitchens for a year now, keeping my eyes and ears open for loose gossip. You two are all anybody's talking about today."

"The kitchen?" Zed whispered. "Did you get Obaachan's message, then?"

"Of course," he replied. He peered around a corner,

then waved them down a deserted corridor to the left.

Their escape route was long, and they had to take a lot of detours. Every time they heard footsteps, the man shunted them into broom closets or behind hanging tapestries until the danger passed. Once he even grabbed a vase of flowers off a decorative table in the hallway and passed it off to the next person he met, concocting some delivery errand as an excuse to send the inconvenient interloper as far away as possible.

After twenty minutes of dodging through corridors, they left the polished and decorated regions of the palace behind and entered the more utilitarian workspaces reserved for palace staff. The man didn't bother to hide them here; all the workers bustling about in their deep purple uniforms were too busy unloading crates or folding linens or chopping onions to notice what anyone else was up to. When they cut through the kitchen, he hastily removed his apron and exchanged it for one of a dozen identical brown woolen cloaks hanging by the back door. He led them out the door, down three steps, and through a covered outdoor pavilion that connected to yet another building.

Twenty long, velvety faces looked up at once. Horses of every color and description stood partitioned into wooden stalls, lazily chewing hay. Their ears swiveled forward as they regarded the newcomers with mild curiosity. One dappled gray horse nickered and shook its mane at them before returning to its breakfast.

Zed started to get worried. He'd never ridden a horse before, and he wasn't particularly excited about making his first attempt in the middle of what was supposed to be a stealthy escape.

"I thought only the Legion used horses," said Tuesday. "Won't we look a bit… obvious?"

The man laughed. "Don't worry, we aren't taking horses. We're just cutting through the stables to get next door."

"What's next door?" asked Zed.

The agent threw open a door at the far end of the aisle and held it open, smiling as Zed and Tuesday passed him. "The garage, of course."

The lights came on automatically as they strolled past a long row of parked hoversleds. Lime-green racing models only large enough for the driver waited next to lumbering gray cargo sleds even larger than Obaachan's. There was even a gold-painted sled decked out in red velvet bunting, with a massive throne built into the base.

"Tyrren's personal hoversled," the man explained, as they hurried past. "For parades and diplomatic visits, mostly. He doesn't actually leave the palace that often."

At last they came to a row of shiny black hoversleds that seemed a bit more practical. Though these medium-sized passenger sleds looked a bit fancier than the models most villagers used, they would definitely draw less attention than any of the others.

"Hop on." The agent selected one and stood at the

controls, waiting for Tuesday and Zed to get settled before activating the sled. It rose from the floor with a gentle hum, then floated along the aisle and out an open bay door into the frigid morning air. They zipped through a circular courtyard, then headed for the back streets out of the city.

"My name's Kenry, by the way." The agent flashed them a grin, then went back to driving.

"Thanks for getting us out of there," said Zed. "Even if we got the door open ourselves, we would never have found the hoversleds on our own."

"My pleasure," he replied. "My cover's blown now—or at least it will be when they realize I've gone missing—but it sounds like we have bigger issues to worry about. I'm looking forward to finally meeting your parents. We have a lot to discuss."

"We're… not sure where they are at the moment," said Tuesday. "For now, we better head back to the safe house and fill the others in on what happened."

"Sure thing. How do we get there?"

Tuesday frowned. "You don't know?" She hadn't memorized enough of Falinnheim's geography yet to know where the palace was, and she and Zed had been asleep on the trip there anyway. But aside from the practical difficulties in giving Kenry directions, something seemed… off. Shouldn't an Operations agent already know all the safehouse locations?

"I mean, *which* safehouse are we going to?" Kenry

elaborated. "There are lots of them. Which village is closest?"

Tuesday let out a breath—that made more sense. She must still be jumpy from dealing with Tyrren and Sylas. "Anduvia."

"I've never been to that one personally, but I think I know the rough location. On the north side of town, right?"

"Sort of northeast, I think," Zed added. "It's near the forest about a quarter league from town."

"No problem," said Kenry. "We'll find it. It's only three leagues from Alexandria to Anduvia. That would take all morning to walk, but by sled it's not even an hour."

They sped over wide, paved roads, past glistening snow-covered fields, and through the outskirts of two other villages before they approached Anduvia. When the smooth pavement changed over to Anduvia's distinctive cobblestones, Kenry left the road and veered southwest until they met the meadow path, which he followed the rest of the way to the cabin.

"What did I tell you?" Kenry said, switching the sled off and allowing it to settle into the snow in front of the safehouse. "No problem at all."

Zed led the way up the cabin's creaky wooden steps. But before he had time to try the knob, the door flew open, and Corvus hurried out to meet them.

"There you two are!" said Corvus breathlessly, standing aside to let them past. "Everyone's been worried to bits— the captain hasn't stopped pacing all night. What happened? And how did you make it back?"

Before they could answer, Corvus caught sight of Kenry coming up the cabin steps behind them. Without a word, he raised one massive fist and punched him right between the eyes.

Kenry stumbled back, then crumpled into snow.

"What are you doing?" Tuesday shrieked. "That's a Resistance agent. He was working undercover in the palace. He helped us escape!"

Corvus lumbered down the steps and stooped over the unconscious figure. "Oh, he's an undercover agent, all right." He flapped open Kenry's cloak, hunting through the pockets. "Just not one of *ours.*"

Corvus found what he was looking for. Zed and Tuesday stared in horror as he held it up to show them, shielding his fingers with a handkerchief.

One pair of leather gloves.

Red.

CHAPTER 17
ALL HANDS ON DECK

"I'm sorry," Zed explained for the thousandth time. "We didn't know who to trust, and this guy was the only one willing to help us, and even if we'd escaped on our own we had no idea where we were or how to get back, and—"

"It's fine," Captain Solomon assured him. "None of this is your fault. We're just glad you're safe. We'll sort out all the rest."

Everyone was gathered around the table in the safehouse cellar. No one bothered to dismiss the kids this time—a meeting this important called for all hands on deck. And besides, there was really no place to send them; Kenry was tied up, blindfolded, and locked in a big empty rutabaga crate upstairs. He was still knocked out, but Corvus had insisted there was no such thing as "too careful" where the Red Hand was involved. They couldn't risk him waking up and overhearing more about their plans than he knew already.

All the adults were careful not to lay blame, but somehow Zed still couldn't swallow his guilt. This safe house might be the very last Resistance stronghold, and they'd managed to lead the bad guys right to it. As though she could feel the disappointment radiating off him, Obaachan chose that moment to lean forward on her makeshift stool and give his shoulder a supportive squeeze.

Not everyone got off so easy. Corvus was willing to admit that, in hindsight, excluding the younger folk from the strategy meetings had been a poor decision. And he couldn't let Orion take all the blame—they'd both failed to notice Tuesday and Zed were missing until their kidnappers were long gone. But that didn't change the fact that Orion had intentionally deceived his superiors about his rogue mission plans.

Pointing out that Obaachan had basically done the same thing didn't help Orion one bit. "She may not follow orders," Corvus had snarled, handing him a scrub brush, "but at least she's honest about it." Orion was put on probation (temporary) and cleaning duty (possibly forever). But the real punishment wasn't washing dishes or scraping the mud off everyone's boots—Fatima was no longer speaking to him. When he'd tried to sit next to her at today's meeting, she'd stormed off to the opposite end of the table. Every time he tried to catch her eye, she made a point of turning away.

"How can he possibly be with the Red Hand?" Tuesday ranted. "Kenry was nothing like them! They're always in pairs, sneaking around like alley rats. They even talk the same—in this eerie, droning voice like they're trying to hypnotize you."

"We don't really know what they're *always* like," said Zed. "We'd only met one set of spies before this, so it was kinda stupid of us to assume they'd all be the same."

"Their leader sure fit the pattern though," Tuesday reminded him. "I've seen bricks with more emotion."

Corvus and Solomon looked over so fast they almost got whiplash. "You know who's leading the Red Hand?"

"Yeah," Tuesday grumped. "A guy called Sylas. Tyrren said he knew our dad, too."

"Wait, you met *Tyrren*?" Dominic interrupted. "*The* Tyrren?"

"What was he like?" Oona wanted to know.

Naomi nodded sagely. "I bet he was stroking an evil pet."

"Probably one of those long-haired, squishy-faced cats," Sakura agreed.

"Or maybe a Fire Serpent," suggested Levi.

"Or a Gabriel Hound," said Fariq.

"Hey, watch it!" Tuesday objected.

Solomon tried to get the meeting back on track. "Start at the beginning. We need to know exactly what happened— every last detail. Anything you learned might be helpful."

Zed pulled out his notebook, jotting down his thoughts while Tuesday talked. By the time she finished recounting their adventure, he was ready with a list of conclusions.

"I don't think Tyrren knows anything about the attack

on the Resistance base," he said. "He wanted Sylas to make holograms of us and show them to the Resistance as proof we were alive. There would be no reason to negotiate if he thought the Resistance leaders had been captured already. And everybody kept calling the Green Fly '*he*,' so I'm pretty sure they don't know it's really the General."

"Something was definitely off," Tuesday agreed. "Sylas tried to make it sound like he only recently learned Mom was back in Falinnheim. But the two Red Hand agents who tried to kidnap her in Kyoto know it's been a lot longer. Either Sylas knows more than he's telling Tyrren, or his agents don't pass everything on to Sylas."

"I'm not sure whether the Red Hand had anything to do with the base attack," said Zed. "Did we learn any more from the other safe houses?"

"We made it back from our scouting mission late last night, but by then you were already missing," Bronwyn reported. She shook her head. "We checked all the hideouts near the base—nothing. It looks like the Research department and the senior students are the only groups who made it out."

"So sitting around waiting for backup has been a giant waste of time," Orion grumbled.

Corvus shot him a silencing glare but let up when Solomon intervened. "Acting before we knew for sure would have been a mistake," the captain concluded, "but the situation has changed. If Tyrren and the Red Hand don't know about the base attack, that means we have a limited window to resolve the situation before they *do* find out. And the fact that so few escaped can work to our advantage; the invaders probably don't realize anyone's missing, and won't be expecting us to strike back. If we can catch them off guard, we might be able to rescue everyone."

"How are we supposed to do that?" asked Skandar.

"I'm open to ideas," said Solomon.

Linus raised his hand. Dominic rolled his eyes and tried to pull his brother's arm back down, but the boy was determined; his arm stayed firmly in the air, his eyes locked on the captain.

Solomon nodded.

"We should wait until the bad guys are sleeping," said Linus fiercely, "then take away their swords and tie them up."

Celia rolled her eyes. "Villains don't have a bedtime, genius."

Solomon ignored her. "Thank you for your contribution, Linus. That's a great idea—they would certainly be easier to beat if they were asleep. I'm afraid we can't count on that, though." He looked up to address the rest of his war council. "How else could we catch them at a disadvantage?"

"If we turned off the power supply, we could surprise them in the dark," suggested Penn.

"Interesting," said Valis, considering. "We only have enough dark vision goggles for the Operations agents though. The rest of you wouldn't be able to see either. Plus, all the lights suddenly going out would alert them we're coming."

"I think it would be better to pick them off one by one," said Amira. "Make as much progress as possible before anyone even realizes we're inside."

"Captain?" said Tuesday, raising her hand. "Do we have any more of those sticky blob things you used to rescue my mom from the Red Hand? That might not be a quiet way to take the soldiers out, but if they can't move, they can't really stop us."

"I'm afraid those were just a prototype," he answered. "Research and Development was still working on a better version."

"We've got half of the scientists right here," Bronwyn pointed out. She turned to the man sitting next to her. "Dev, do you know anything about the weapons prototypes in development?"

"Me?" he asked, startled. "I'm a botanist. I study plants; I don't know anything about weapons. You'd need a chemist or a materials engineer for that. There's no such thing as a plain old 'scientist,' you know—we specialize."

"I wish there was some way we could see what's going on in there," Fatima sighed. "*Before* we try to break back in, I mean."

Tuesday gave up pretending—she had more serious problems to worry about than keeping other dimensions a secret. "Do you really not have *any* way of communicating long distance?" she asked Solomon. "Like a cell phone?"

He frowned. "You mean like the intercom system? Or

the security monitors? Those only work inside the base. We don't have any way of connecting to them from here."

"What about those crystal ball things?" she insisted. "I've seen them used to tell time and get directions and share duty schedules. I even saw one play a recording of a Resistance agent interviewing Scrimbley! Couldn't we use them to talk to someone inside the base? I bet the General has one in her pocket right now."

Penn spoke up. "If anyone knows the spheres' capabilities, it's Neri here—after all, she invented them." He turned to the scientist to his left. "What do you think?"

Neri shook her head. "The spheres can store recordings, but the information stays on the sphere that collected it. There isn't a way to transfer information between them. I don't know of *any* device that can communicate across long distances."

"I do!" Zed realized aloud.

Tuesday rolled her eyes. "Yeah, me too. Lots of them. But all the cell phones and radios and TVs and walkie-talkies in the world can't help us when they're stuck in another dimension."

"Not stuff from home," he explained, ignoring everyone's confused looks. "The holograms, remember? Mom reprogrammed them to recite a coded message when we said the right passwords. It worked on holograms all over Persepolis. Maybe the ones in other cities too—I'm not sure."

"How's that supposed to help?" Orion grumped.

"Our whole problem is not knowing what's going on inside the base right now. We don't have direct contact with anyone inside, but maybe we could use a hologram to do the talking for us."

"That might just work," said Neri. "The base's hologram receptionist uses the security monitors and intercom system to do her job. If we had a way to get into the hologram's programming, we could use her as our spy on the inside!"

"Fascinating," Corvus said. "Do you know how your mother accessed the holograms?"

"No," Zed admitted. "But I know someone who does."

———

There was no way around it; they had to abandon the safe house. Captain Solomon was firm on that point. Even though they had the spy locked up, the fact that anyone outside the Resistance knew the cabin's location made it too risky to keep using. "It's fortunate Corvus acted so quickly," he'd explained, clapping his lieutenant on the shoulder. "His cover is blown now, of course, but he stopped the spy from seeing anyone else."

That left the matter of what to do with Kenry. Amira argued they shouldn't pass up the opportunity to interrogate him—they'd never gotten their hands on a Red Hand agent before, after all. But again, the captain decided the risk was too great. Any information they managed to get out of him would probably be a lie, and he'd learn too much about the Resistance in the attempt. Instead they loaded his crate onto the stolen palace hoversled, Bronwyn driving while the rest walked to Anduvia in strict silence (again, preventing Kenry from gleaning anything useful from overheard conversations.) Bronwyn parked the sled in front of a busy brick storefront in the center of town, as though she was delivering a crate of supplies, then casually strolled away. By the time any of the villagers thought to check the label—*CAUTION: THIS MAN IS AN AGENT OF THE RED HAND*—she'd joined the others in the back room of Cordelia's Apothecary.

"Somehow, I thought you'd be harder to find," Valis told Scrimbley. They had planned to have the children wait with Fatima while the rest of the adults split up and scoured the market for signs of thievery, but when they arrived in the alley behind the apothecary he was leaning against the door frame, waiting for them.

"Scrimbley's got a sixth sense," Tuesday said, glowering at the smuggler as Solomon passed him a bundle of coins. "He can *smell* when there's money to be made."

"I still don't trust him," Celia complained. "How do we know he's not working with the Red Hand? Pretty big coincidence they knew right where to find us last night, don't you think?"

"As I said before," Scrimbley explained, dropping the money bag into his cloak pocket with a satisfying *clink*, "rule number one is 'look out for Number One.' I got *standards,* see? Dealing with the Red Hand would be a losing business proposition. Ain't got a shred of common decency about 'em. They don't negotiate, they don't show no appreciation, and they don't pay."

He made himself comfortable on a stack of boxes and propped his feet up on Cordelia's worktable. "Enough about those skunks. Let's get down to business. You're looking for a way into the hologram system?"

Solomon explained what they hoped to do in the most general terms, carefully sidestepping any mention of trouble at the Resistance base. Scrimbley related how he'd connected Zed and Tuesday's parents with an employee in the service department at Hololab Industries, who was able to add a few new tricks to the holograms' programming. He was sure he'd learned enough from watching over the technician's shoulder to repeat the maneuver. "But I'd have to get my hands on the hardware, you understand. That trick only worked because all the hologram stations in Persepolis were wired together. We can't talk to your receptionist from here."

"Would access to a security panel on the outside of the base be enough?" Corvus asked.

"Should be. But I'll need the right equipment. I can scrounge up a display tablet and some connection cables right here in Anduvia's market, no problem." He looked meaningfully at Solomon.

Solomon sighed and pulled another bag of coins from his cloak.

Scrimbley flashed him a gap-toothed grin. "Pleasure doing business with you, as always, Your Captainship."

175

CHAPTER 18
BACK TO THE BASE

Obaachan's part in the plan was easy. They'd crammed all the supplies they could manage onto her cargo sled before abandoning the safehouse, so while everyone else was in Anduvia, she headed off to deliver them to the empty hideout on the base's southeast side. Corvus sent Fiona with a coded message tied to her leg, instructing Resistance contacts from the nearby village to join Obaachan and wait for more instructions. "She knows where to go," Corvus assured them. "Fiona takes messages to the Tilford Heath outpost all the time."

At first, Solomon had assumed Professor Orpin and the students would follow Obaachan, but that kicked up an immediate cloud of outrage. Celia and Dominic protested they were nearly old enough for apprenticeships; if they chose the Operations division, they'd be doing this sort of thing all the time. Tuesday complained that she and Zed had already dealt with soldiers and the secret police on numerous occasions, and had now added Tyrren himself to the list, so it was a bit late to insist they couldn't handle it. Fariq diplomatically pointed out that the plan was mostly Zed's to begin with, so it wasn't exactly fair to leave him out now. Professor Orpin insisted he wasn't waiting around to get ambushed again; since Solomon's agents were the only ones with either combat training or weapons, he'd be sticking with them. Fatima suggested that the children could help provide a cover story for their journey—if anyone asked, they could (nearly honestly) say they were escorting a bunch of students on a field trip.

"All right!" said Solomon at last. "At least this way we can keep an eye on you. But you'll do exactly as you're told, understood? No daring heroics or last-minute scheming. Just stick close and let the adults take care of things."

All the kids slapped on their most compliant faces. Of course they'd be good. Naturally! How could he ever suspect otherwise?

Since they'd had to park the palace's hoversled in Anduvia to get rid of Kenry, and Obaachan had already taken hers, everyone else had to walk the three leagues back to the base. For the first couple of hours they followed paved roads; agents, scientists, and schoolkids alike, they chatted and laughed and passed sticks of jerky and wayfarer's biscuits back and forth. But when they neared the base, Corvus led them off the road and into the wintery meadow, walking single file to tamp down a path through the ankle-deep snow. Their approach to the foot of the mountain had to be precise, following blind spots in the base surveillance system, in case the invaders were using it to check for an ambush.

Tuesday spent the entire journey shooting dark sideways glances at Scrimbley, who was tromping cheerfully through the snow, alternately gnawing on sticks of jerky and whistling some tune she didn't recognize. Usually, she trusted Captain Solomon's judgment, and even his most cautious agents had agreed they had no alternative if they wanted Scrimbley's help—they had to bring the smuggler with them to the base. Tuesday couldn't manage to shake her suspicion. Her mother always said she trusted Scrimbley's good nature, even if it was buried under a layer of nervous self-preservation instincts. He wasn't a bad person, Mom had insisted—it's just that his definitions of right and wrong were a bit off-kilter. But Tuesday couldn't forgive so easily. After all, Mom wasn't the one Scrimbley had double crossed, sending soldiers to her house to kidnap her (and then expecting her undying gratitude when he rescued the victims of his own disaster.) And Solomon hadn't come out on the losing end of one of the smuggler's bargains yet. They'd think twice about trusting their fate to Scrimbley once he betrayed them personally. And he *would*—Tuesday was sure of it. It was only a matter of time.

They snaked along the northwest foot of the mountain until Corvus stopped at a control panel hidden in the crevice behind a boulder. "It's all yours," he said, waving Scrimbley forward.

Scrimbley fished the connecting cables from the bag slung over his shoulder and hooked an electronic tablet up to the panel. Everyone gathered around Scrimbley, standing on tiptoes and peeking over shoulders, all vying for a glimpse at the screen. At first a string of green rune-like symbols cascaded down the surface, scrolling too rapidly to read them. The screen blinked twice, went black for a few seconds, blinked again. Then the hologram receptionist's round, cheery bronze face appeared.

Linus waved at her. "Hi, Miss Erma!"

"She can't hear you," Fariq informed him. "Or see you."

"Plus she's not even a real person," Celia added.

But Linus just grinned. "I don't care. I'm happy to see her anyway."

Solomon leaned closer to give Scrimbley instructions, which he typed into the tablet. Erma responded as though they were standing face to face, having a conversation. After verifying some security phrases to confirm she really was talking to Captain Solomon, she was happy to tell him everything she knew.

"Three days ago a group dressed in mining uniforms came up the mountain road from Kyoto. They arrived at the export staging bay and tried to enter the crystal mine unnoticed. When the export bay supervisor asked for their security clearance, they pulled out weapons and barged through. The security team guarding the mine exit were taken hostage. The intruders tried to force the hostages to lead them to the Green Fly, but one of them managed to hit an emergency alarm button, which activated the door shields. The invaders got up the stairs and to the main hallway before the doorways sealed. Their hostages escaped in the chaos and locked themselves in the kitchen. All base occupants are sheltering in the rooms they occupied at the time the doors sealed."

"Except us," muttered Dominic.

"We're not 'base occupants' at the moment," Professor Orpin reminded him.

"How many intruders?" Solomon asked Scrimbley, who typed the questions out to Erma. "How are they armed? Where are they now?"

Erma relayed the answers: ten intruders, still dressed in miners' gear, were patrolling the hallways in pairs. Each had one shape-shifting weapon, which they had changed from battle axes to battering rams (and everything in between) trying to break into the sealed rooms. They'd put some pretty good dents in the barriers to the officers' lounge and the dining hall, but so far had not made it through any of them. When brute force failed, they started yelling at the doorways, demanding the Green Fly surrender. (Which wasn't terribly effective, since they didn't have any hostages to negotiate with.) They didn't seem to know their way around the base, since they were addressing doors at random.

Solomon took a moment to digest the information. "Shape shifting swords…" he muttered. "That means we're dealing with the Legion, then. Or at least some of them."

"*Good*," Corvus growled. "I've been waiting for a chance to cross swords with those thugs."

"If one regiment of the Legion acted alone, then Tyrren and the Red Hand might not know anything about it," said Valis hopefully.

Zed frowned. "Everyone's been trapped for three days? They must be starving."

"All living quarters, offices, and duty stations store a week's worth of emergency rations for their maximum occupancy," Fatima explained. "I'm sure everyone's bored, and uncomfortable, and worried. But as long as the soldiers can't get to them, they're all right."

"Rations…" Amira repeated. "The intruders might have the advantage at the moment, but in a way, they're stuck too. They've spent three days trying to patrol the entire base with only a handful of soldiers, so they can't spare anyone to go back to Kyoto. And it sounds like they can't get into the kitchens or greenhouse. I wonder what they're doing about food?"

Scrimbley relayed the question to Erma, who reported they'd been surviving on water flasks and wayfarer's biscuits. "And based on all the grumbling," she added with a smirk, "it looks like their supplies are running out."

The captain turned around to address his forces. "This is the best news we could have hoped for. Based on the conditions inside, here's how we'll proceed: Scrimbley will stay here, giving Erma instructions. She can use the intercom system one room at a time to find out where the General is and get her up to speed on the plan. Corvus and Bronwyn will escort the scientists back through the escape hatch to the lab, where they'll collect anything we could use as a distraction or a makeshift weapon. The rest of the agents will take on the soldiers. Professor Orpin, you and the students will stay here with Scrimbley."

Celia and Tuesday protested almost in unison. "What?"

"That wasn't our deal!"

"We can help you!"

"I'm not going anywhere without one of the agents," said Professor Orpin again. "What if the soldiers try to escape, and come out and find us here? We'd be sitting ducks!"

"Well that makes me feel *loads* better about my job," Scrimbley muttered. "I *have* to stay here."

Everyone ignored him.

Solomon was usually the poster child for calm, level-headed leadership. But apparently his well of patience had finally run dry. "This isn't a game!" he said, exasperated. "You are *children*. Adults have a duty to keep you from harm. I don't care if it seems unfair—I'm not about to send you in there with violent, armed intruders. And if your families were here, they'd say the same thing. Being safe is far more important than feeling included."

"We won't get caught!" Tuesday insisted. "We'll be careful."

"*Caught?*" Solomon repeated. "You and Zed have been

lucky so far, but the Legion is ruthless. You really think getting caught is all you have to worry about? And even if they settled for capture, instead of killing you on the spot, what would that accomplish? If the soldiers announced they had you as hostages, what would your parents do next, do you think? They would surrender *immediately* if they thought it would protect you—you know they would. And so would your grandmother. Don't put them in danger just so you can feel brave."

Tuesday sighed, defeated. Solomon was right, of course. She would just have to make peace with being treated like inconvenient luggage. But then, to her surprise, Orion stepped forward.

"Let me take charge of them, Captain."

Corvus eyed him dubiously. "Yeah, that worked out just *great* last time."

"Look, I know I messed up!" Orion argued. "I get that. Give me a chance to make it right. The professor's got a point—leaving them *anywhere* without an armed escort is risky. I could take them into the maintenance tunnels. We can keep an eye on things from behind the geothermal grates; the soldiers will never even know we're there."

Solomon appraised him in silence for a moment. Finally, he nodded.

Corvus stooped down so he could whisper directly into Orion's face. "We're counting on you, agent. Don't screw this up."

CHAPTER 19
SOME UNEXPECTED ALLIES

The teams parted, each heading for the door Erma had opened for them by overriding the security lockdown. Corvus and Bronwyn escorted the scientists up the tunnel leading to the lab, their massive knives already drawn. Solomon, Valis, and Amira hiked up the mountain toward the secret entrance tucked behind a waterfall. And Orion led the school kids and their teacher around the foot of the mountain to an emergency exit that connected with the crystal mine. "We can access the geothermal tunnels from the mine," he explained, "which will lead into the base's ventilation system. The soldiers will never think to look for anyone there, as long as we're quiet. And there's a chance we could access the sealed rooms from the vents—maybe smuggle some more people out if…"

He didn't finish the sentence, but Tuesday understood.

No point jinxing the plan by casting doubt on its chances of success. Especially since they were forbidden to actually help.

"On that note," Professor Orpin announced, "It's time for a game."

Everyone groaned. They knew what was coming. Their teacher must have picked this trick up from Professor Nigume, who taught the little kids. Professor Orpin was apparently oblivious to the fact that his older students saw right through the charade, because he kept trying to use the Quiet Game on them. Even *Linus* was too old to be fooled by the Quiet Game.

Still… things were different this time. The prospect of "winning" the game might have lost its appeal, but they weren't usually hiding from sword-toting ruffians bent on revenge. This time, *losing* could have immediate and severe consequences. Zed nodded dutifully at Tuesday. She rolled her eyes, but joined him in miming zipping up their lips and throwing away the key.

The emergency door around the side of the mountain was waiting open for them, just as Erma had promised. Crystals lining the rough-hewn walls slowly glowed to life as Orion led his charges single-file through the tunnel. Their path sloped gradually upward as it connected with various fingers of the mining operation, then dead-ended at a collection of metal ladders embedded into the cave wall. Orion didn't have a pocket sphere to pull up a map, but apparently he didn't need one; he immediately started up the third ladder, as confident about his chosen path as if the maintenance tunnels were part of his daily commute.

After several minutes of climbing, Orion clambered into one of the horizontal shafts intersecting the ladder. This one was also rough stone, but much smaller than the cavernous mining tunnels below them. Linus could just barely walk upright in this one, and everyone else had to stoop to avoid hitting their heads. Tall, lanky Professor Orpin was nearly bent double.

It was also darker than the previous tunnels; there were plenty of jagged crystals jutting out of the walls, but these didn't glow. The only light leaked through a series of metal grates set into the wall, spaced out every twenty steps or so. Orion paused for a moment to peer through the first grate he reached, but he quickly crept on. He couldn't explain what he'd seen beyond it without breaking his vow of silence, so each person lined up behind him stopped for their own peek into what turned out to be a janitor's closet. The security lockdown must have also interrupted the automated sanitation schedule, because a dozen robotic cleaning pods were lined up against the wall, waiting in their charging stations. Normally, by this time in the afternoon they'd still be busy vacuuming, mopping, and polishing the base's floors.

The group went on, pausing to check each grate they passed, but none of the rooms were occupied. At least, not occupied by *people*. As they approached the sixth grate on their procession through the ventilation shafts, muffled sounds wafted toward them. The closer they crept, the more distinct the disgruntled muttering became. Fariq was next in line behind Orion, and as he reached the grate, he beckoned to the kids behind him to gather around for a better look.

They had reached the poultry wing. Though the grate was set at face height in their tunnel, it looked out onto the dirt floor of the birds' arena, where chickens and dodos were milling aimlessly about, occasionally scratching and pecking at the ground in a fruitless search for anything edible they'd overlooked.

"Poor things," Oona whispered. "No one's been able to come feed them for days."

"You lost the Quiet Game!" Linus blurted out.

"So did you," Fariq whispered back.

"Now *you* lost too!" Linus retorted.

Celia rolled her eyes. "The whole 'game' was stupid anyway."

From his place at the back of the line, Professor Orpin craned his neck toward the knot of kids around the grate. "What's the holdup?" he hissed.

It didn't matter how boring the Quiet Game had seemed earlier; no one was about to pass up this opportunity. Every kid in line turned back to point an accusing finger at their teacher.

"Ha!" said Linus (who, having already lost, was no longer

bound by the "rules.") "Now *you* lost the game, Professor!"

It didn't really matter; there were no people in this room to hear them. And even if the soldiers happened to be outside the door at this very moment, there was no way they could hear anything over the birds' clucking and the droning ventilation fans set into the ceiling.

"There's nothing we can do for them," Orion said, trying to break up the traffic jam and get things moving again. "If there were people inside, they might be able to pry the grate off and let us in, but we'd need a screwdriver to open it from this side."

Luckily, Zed just happened to have a screwdriver strapped to his arm. Or at least, he would in a minute. He rolled back the sleeve of his cloak and grasped the slipsteel bracer, which melted into his grip and solidified as a crude screwdriver. This tool was much less intricate than a key, so it only took a couple of tries to match the notches of the screws holding the panel in place. He ignored the shocked exclamations of the other kids, who had not yet seen his father's converted umbrella in action, and pushed the freed panel aside.

"Well, aren't you just full of surprises!" said Orion proudly. After shooing aside the curious birds that had come to investigate this new development, he laced his fingers together to make a foothold and hoisted the kids one by one through the hole. Professor Orpin came last, then turned around and pulled Orion up after him.

They were immediately mobbed by hungry birds, all flapping and clucking at the newcomers in hopes of a handout. One of the bolder dodos even stuck its head through the open grate hole in search of snacks, forcing the professor to replace the metal cover before the bird could tumble inside.

"This is as safe a place to wait as any," said Orion, appraising their latest hideout. "The outer doors are sealed, and there's more room to stretch out. And if there's any trouble, we can always duck back into the tunnel."

Fariq and Oona headed for the supply closet with their feathery fan club in eager pursuit. "Come on, birdies," Fariq crooned. "Let's get you something tasty."

"Wait!" Tuesday called. "Don't feed them yet."

"Why not?" asked Oona.

Tuesday didn't answer her. "Can we talk to Erma from in here?" she asked Orion.

"Sure. Why?"

"I think I know a way we can help the captain, while still keeping our promise to stay out of danger. But it would involve having Erma release the door shields on this room for a minute."

He gave her a shrewd look. "What's that got to do with feeding the birds?"

"The captain said the scientists were looking for things they could use to cause a distraction so his agents could catch the soldiers off guard. So I figured—"

Zed broke into a grin. "I think I know where this is going…"

"I get it!" Celia interrupted. "That might actually work."

Tuesday beamed at Orion. "What could possibly be more distracting than a parade?"

———

They couldn't see her—Erma's hologram only showed up at the projector built into her desk—but when Orion called for the receptionist, her voice floated down from the intercom speaker in the ceiling. Erma passed the message on to Corvus and Bronwyn in the laboratory, who signed off on the plan and added a few suggestions of their own. Fariq and Oona passed out shields from the supply room, and everyone herded the birds back to their coop so Orion could prepare the first wave of attack.

After confirming all the soldiers were busy patrolling other wings of the base, Erma instructed the security system to raise the metal slats covering the poultry wing doors. This allowed Orion to sneak off to the janitor's closet down the hall and return with their secret weapons: a dozen metal buckets, the entire flock of robotic cleaning pods, and a barrel containing a year's supply of dental beads.

"I didn't bring this up at the safehouse meeting," Orion explained as he and Tuesday scooped dental beads into the buckets and balanced them on top of the domed pods. "But you remember those sticky blob weapons you asked the captain about? He commissioned those from the

Research department himself. Said he got the idea from a dormitory prank he was assigned to investigate."

"Solomon said he used up all the blobs though," Tuesday reminded him.

"That's true. And it's a shame, really, because they would have been perfect. But I figure we can do the next best thing: recreate the prank."

Tuesday vaguely recalled reading something about a problem in the men's dorm when she had "borrowed" a classified report to help plan her escape from the base. But that was back before she'd learned her parents were in Falinnheim too, and had been trying to find a way into the Resistance stronghold at the exact same time she and Zed were looking for a way out of it.

Zed, Levi, and Dominic hauled sacks of poultry feed from the supply room and used a roll of twine to strap one bag to the back of each cleaning pod. Not that they had a back or front, or any features at all, really; the mechanics inside were covered by domed barrels of slick metal sheeting, about waist high to an adult and just wide enough for one person to wrap their arms around. It was actually pretty tricky to keep the bags from sliding down, but after some trial and error Levi worked out a way of knotting the twine into a sort of harness that worked pretty well. Then they wheeled the pods into a line in front of the doors to the hall, each balancing a bucket of dental beads on its "head" and carrying a backpack full of bird snacks.

"On three," Orion called to the team holding the birds back. "One… two…" He turned each of the pods to the mop setting, then used his knife to make a tiny slash in each of the grain sacks. "Three!"

Zed and Dominic opened the doors. The cleaning robots took off down the hall, sprinkling feed pellets from their leaky backpacks as they went. Professor Orpin and the rest of his students moved their shields aside, releasing a wave of hungry chickens and dodos, who scampered after the robots. When the entire flock made it into the hall, Zed and Dominic closed the poultry wing doors behind them, and Orion instructed Erma to lock the door shields back in place.

"Erma, please display the hallway security feed," said Orion.

Everyone crowded into the supply room for a look at the screen mounted on the wall. It blinked to life, showing an overhead view of the robots' progress through the halls. They were rocketing along at their highest speed setting, chased by an angry mob of chickens and dodos competing for the feed pellets dropped along the way. Every time the procession passed out of one camera's range, it dropped off the screen to be replaced by the next video feed down the hall. Past the kitchens, dining hall, repair bay, and officers' lounge; around a corner to the residence wing, then up the next corridor by the classrooms and library; the cleaning pods led the poultry parade through half the base before they encountered the first pair of soldiers.

The soldiers drew their weapons, but it was too late—the pods encircled them, slowing to a prowling crawl to corral them in. The dodos caught up first, surrounding the cleaning pods to gorge on the ring of dropped pellets. The chickens followed, pecking between the dodos' legs for their share of the feast. The soldiers trapped inside looked surprised, but not worried—sure, they were outnumbered, but what match are a few robots and birds for shapeshifting weapons?

Zed winced as he watched the soldiers transform their slipsteel batons into massive broadswords. He knew the dodos were destined to be eaten eventually, but somehow, it didn't seem fair to have them slaughtered on his account. The cleaning robots weren't alive to begin with, but there was something endearing about them, too. The plan had seemed so clever only a few minutes ago, but now the sickening realization settled in—they had sent pawns to fight in their place, and the enemy would show them no mercy.

The soldiers raised their swords.

"Release the water tanks!" Orion called to the ceiling.

Erma must have access to the cleaning pods' programming, because at that moment the robots stopped circling and flooded the hallway with mop water. The soldiers took this opportunity to launch their attack, which put pretty decent dents in a couple of the robots. But they knocked over the buckets balanced on top in the process.

Thousands of dental beads cascaded to the floor,

dissolving in the puddles and then billowing out into a thick cloud of foamy toothpaste. It swallowed the soldiers' feet, then their knees, and kept right on building. When it reached their waists, they started to panic, slicing at the foam with their swords, which of course had no effect at all (other than fluffing up the toothpaste volcano even higher). The chickens and dodos edged away from the spreading suds but kept right on eating.

"It's even more spectacular than I imagined," said Orion fondly as he watched the chaos unfold. "I didn't get to watch the first time."

"What are you talking about?" asked Dominic. "It was Tuesday's plan. And Tuesday got the idea from Captain Solomon's invention."

"True," he admitted, a mischievous grin spreading over his face. "But where do you think the captain got the idea?"

"The dormitory prank!" Tuesday realized. "That was *you*?"

Orion took a bow.

CHAPTER 20
ONWARD!

Two down, eight to go. The toothpaste volcano wouldn't hold the soldiers forever, of course; it was only meant as a diversion. But the diversion seemed to be working, because right on cue two new soldiers appeared on the security feed, dashing around the corner to investigate the commotion.

"What in Hades' hairnet is going on?" one of the newcomers yelled.

The pair trapped in the suds tried to fight their way out of the ring of robots, but they kept slipping off their feet and landing face-first in the foam, which left them too busy spluttering and wiping their eyes to hold a conversation. Without warning, the robots broke formation and advanced toward the new soldiers, trailing streaks of multicolored goop in their wake.

Cleaning pods never made noise or flashing lights, and they definitely didn't carry weapons. There was really no reason for anyone to be afraid of them, let alone two burly men with swords. But something about the silent, coordinated persistence of a dozen robotic mops was threatening enough to override the soldiers' logic for a moment. The men changed their swords into a battle-axe and a spear and backed warily away. Behind them, Erma retracted the shields on the door to an empty office. The soldiers must not have known the room was empty though—perhaps they assumed whoever was inside had finally decided to surrender—because when they went inside to investigate, the robots swarmed in and blocked the door closed behind them. The curtain of metal slats fell back down, then solidified in place, trapping the soldiers inside.

Back in the poultry wing, the spectators cheered.

"Good thinking, Erma!" said Linus.

Orion instructed Erma to send the cleaning pods on to the next two soldiers, and the poultry parade marched along behind. The noisy procession only made it to the next hallway before they found them: a saber-toting woman and a man with a massive sledgehammer stormed up the corridor to meet them.

"We used up all the dental beads on the first two!" Zed realized. "What are the robots supposed to do now?"

"Don't worry," said Orion, staring intensely at the screen. "I've got a few more tricks up my sleeve."

The shields slid off of the door to their right, but the soldiers didn't take the bait this time. They charged at the incoming line of cleaning pods, raising their weapons overhead. But just as they were about to collide, Orion instructed the pods to spin on the spot, and then retreat. The force of the spin flung bird feed out of the leaking sacks, showering the soldiers. And then the dodos surged forward, biting the soldiers' shins and ankles in an effort to dig out the pellets caught in the cuffed hems of their mining coveralls.

Once again, Zed prepared himself for the dodos to meet a gruesome end. And once again, the plucky birds managed to surprise him. The woman changed her saber into something resembling a tennis racket and attempted to swat the nearest dodo away from her legs. The dodo responded by hopping out of the way and biting her on the wrist, which made her drop the weapon. The moment she released it the racket morphed back into a plain silvery rod, hit the floor with a *clank,* and rolled away in the forest of scaly, clawed feet. Her partner tried the same maneuver, but he forgot to transform his weapon first, so all he managed to accomplish was whacking his own feet with a sledgehammer before dropping it into the feathery stampede.

The soldiers were so busy yelling at each other and kicking at the swarming birds that they didn't even notice the science squad had arrived.

Corvus led the attack. He lowered his head behind one massive arm, his elbow raised to protect his face, and charged at the soldiers like a rhinoceros. The woman was knocked to the ground and immediately swarmed by hungry dodos. Her partner kept his feet, but the impact sent him stumbling into the office Erma had left open earlier. The hologram wasted no time slamming the barriers shut behind him.

Bronwyn dove into the dodos to retrieve the other soldier before she got pecked to bits. She rose from the torrent of feathers a moment later with the woman pinned in a wrestler's headlock. Fatima and Penn secured the soldier's hands with electrical tape, and then accompanied Bronwyn as she marched her captive over to the base's detention wing.

By this time all the birds were too frazzled to move on to the next target, so a couple of the scientists removed the sacks from the cleaning pods and spread the pellets on the floor so they could eat in peace. Then Corvus instructed Erma to send the cleaning pods on to the next pair of soldiers, while his crew doubled back through the corridors to sneak up on them from behind.

The cleaning pods didn't have any dental beads left to trap the soldiers with, and they'd used up all their water reserves, so they couldn't even flood the hallways to make the path slippery. But a coordinated line of robotic mops that seemed to have a mind of their own was apparently enough of a distraction all by itself, because when the cleaning pods encountered their next target, they had the soldiers' undivided attention.

While the soldiers stalked toward the advancing robots, Corvus and the scientists rushed in from behind with a bunch of glass vials filled with coarse green powder. They lobbed the vials down the hall, smashing them open on the floor, which released their contents in a cloud of greenish dust. The soldiers turned around to face this new attack, but they couldn't do much; the moment they stepped into the cloud, they collapsed in a furious sneezing fit.

"Take that!" yelled Dev, lobbing more vials at the soldiers. "Powdered leaves of *Achillea ptarmica*—better known as sneezewort!"

Soon a new pair of soldiers ran in from an adjoining hall to join the party. The robots couldn't do much about this except line up to block their hallway, but that still left two escape routes open.

The scientists were decked out in all the protective gear the lab had to offer, which turned out to be good thinking; rubber gloves, splash goggles, and clear face shields might not seem like they'd be much use against swords, but they allowed the scientists to keep using their sneezewort grenades without being affected themselves. It was a temporary victory, though; the soldiers soon figured out they could escape the worst of the cloud's effects by pulling their shirt collars over their noses and charging straight through it. Corvus lunged between the scientists and the advancing soldiers, his knife held at the ready, but it was four against one—Corvus wouldn't be able to hold them off forever.

Orion stared hungrily at the screen. "I was afraid things

would come down to this. I should be there to help! But I promised the captain I wouldn't leave you alone…"

"But I didn't…" Professor Orpin muttered to himself.

"Didn't what?" asked Orion.

"I didn't promise to stay out of harm's way." He laughed bitterly. "I practically *begged* to, but I didn't promise. You have to stay here and protect the students, but I'm just tagging along. In fact, sometimes I feel like I've spent my entire life just tagging along. I think it's time I got involved, for once." As the professor spoke, a determined glint grew in his eyes. They stopped darting nervously around and locked on the chaos unfolding on the view screen.

"Look," Orion protested, "no one's happier than I am to see your backbone's finally growing in, but you couldn't have picked a worse moment for it. What do you expect to do against four professional thugs and an infinitely rotating arsenal?"

"Uh…" Levi interrupted, pointing at the screen, "make that *six* professional thugs."

Two more soldiers stormed up behind the robot blockade, leaving a trail of sudsy boot prints. Apparently, the cleaning pods' first victims had worked their way out of the toothpaste trap.

"Where is Captain Solomon's team?" Orion called to the ceiling.

"The captain has not yet entered any area patrolled by the security system," Erma reported.

"Blast. They must still be climbing up to the waterfall entrance. Corvus and his team need reinforcements *now.*"

"What about my parents?" Tuesday suggested. "Nyx could go help if Mom told her what to do or asked her to protect someone specific. And my dad's had all the same combat training as the soldiers."

Orion shook his head. "When the soldiers broke in, they demanded to see the General, not your father. They might not know he's at the base to begin with. And we're not sure if they realize your mother is the missing regent. If the Legion managed to capture either of them... no, it's just too risky."

Professor Orpin turned to Zed. "Your slipsteel tool— that's your father's sword, correct?"

There was no point trying to hide it anymore. Zed nodded. "It won't be a sword for anyone else, though. That's really brave of you to want to go help, Professor, but—"

"It's not for me," he interrupted. "I might not be able to use it, but I could deliver it to the one person who can."

"You... want to take it to my dad?" Zed couldn't believe his ears. It was so unlike his teacher to take any chances at all—Professor Orpin normally wouldn't dare to wear mismatched socks, let alone run into the middle of a battle.

"Weren't you listening?" Orion huffed. "Their father's spent three days in lockdown trying to *avoid* the intruders. Why waste it by blowing his cover now?"

"Shouldn't that be his decision?" the professor

countered. "We're wasting time! The researchers aren't fighters either, but they were willing to stick their necks out for the rest of us. It's time I returned the favor."

He didn't wait around for further argument. Orpin held his hand out to Zed, who melted the bracer off his arm and handed it over.

Erma confirmed that Beren, Theadora, Nyx, and the General were in the conference chambers near the reception area. But since there were no geothermal shafts in the center of the base, the ventilation ducts connecting to it would be too small to crawl through. Orpin's only option was to pass through the hallways, unprotected, and hope he didn't meet any soldiers on the way. So that's exactly what he did. Erma raised the shields from the poultry wing just long enough to let him through, and without a word, he pelted down the hall.

Everyone crowded back into the supply room to watch the security feed. The screen flicked from one view to the next as the professor sped past each camera, finally arriving at the reception area at the heart of the base. Erma's hologram offered him a jaunty salute as he ran past her desk, but he didn't return the gesture; just one more hallway, and he'd be at the General's conference chamber.

And that's when the last two soldiers showed up.

Orpin skidded around the corner to find a man and woman in mining coveralls charging toward him from the other end of the long corridor. The conference chamber lay halfway between them. He sprinted forward, his stork-like legs covering the distance in fewer strides than the soldiers, but his opponents were quick too. It was like watching an impending train wreck in slow motion; if something didn't change soon, it looked like they were going to collide right in front of the General's door.

"I can't watch!" squealed Oona, peeking at the viewscreen from between her fingers.

"Come on…" urged Dominic tensely, "you can make it, Professor… "

They were ten meters apart, then five, then two—

And then Professor Orpin tripped.

He dropped to the floor, landing on his backside with his legs splayed out in front of him. The soldiers swung their swords where his neck had been milliseconds earlier, instead slicing through empty air as he slid past their knees. Just when it looked like the professor was about to crumple into the wall, the shields raised from the doorway to his left, revealing the interior door was already open. Orpin kept right on sliding, one leg stretched out in front of him like a runner stealing home base, and sailed straight through the empty doorway.

He chucked the slipsteel bracer into the air.

And a hand reached out and caught it.

The poultry wing exploded with cheers as Zed and Tuesday watched their father leap into the hall on his good foot, the bracer melting smoothly into a circular shield in his grip. A flaming blur sailed over Professor Orpin's head as Nyx bounded out to join him, and then the doorway sealed itself behind them.

The soldiers retreated a few steps to assess the situation. Then they transformed their swords into a pair of identical silver planks, which they held out horizontally so they blocked the entire hallway. In unison, they rammed forward, attempting to push their opponents back or knock them down, but Nyx jumped out in front and created a wall of blue fire that nearly kissed the ceiling. The soldier's planks sprouted long handles, allowing them to wield their barricades from a safe distance, but when they attempted to shove them through the flames the entire length glowed red as the heat traveled up the handles and into their palms.

The soldiers swore and dropped their scalding-hot weapons, which reverted into silver batons in midair and clanked to the floor. Nyx created a gap in her curtain of flames, and Beren's shield shot forward as a long, thin, arm with an overturned box at the end. The box slapped down over one of the batons and the arm retracted through the fire wall, pulling the inactive weapon along with it.

The other soldier managed to kick her weapon out of the way before Beren could snatch it, and now she picked it up in her left hand while blowing on the burning welt seared into her right.

"Coward!" she spat, morphing the slipsteel cylinder into a massive saber. "Enough playing around—turn that contraption back into a proper sword and let's finish this."

Beren just laughed. "You have no imagination, Malena. That sword you're holding can become the perfect tool for every situation, but you can't get past thinking of it as a weapon."

The woman scowled, but went back to examining her burned palm.

Her partner sneered. "Why don't you come out here and face us instead of hiding behind that mutt? Or would you rather run away, as usual?"

"I'll protect the people that need me by any means necessary," replied Beren calmly. "Stand and fight, or strategic retreat—makes no difference to me. My pride will never be more important than the mission. Things might have turned out very differently if you'd learned that, all those years ago. But I guess you still haven't learned." He picked up the confiscated baton and slipped it into his pocket.

"Looks like you're still carrying around that souvenir you got battling Nicodemus," the soldier tried next, gesturing at the bandaged foot Beren held gingerly off the ground. "How about we make it a matching set?"

"Looks like you two have a matching set of souvenirs yourselves," Beren retorted. "You'll be remembering this Royal Guard reunion party for *weeks*."

They might have gone on trash talking forever, but at that moment Solomon, Valis, and Amira arrived. They dashed up the hallway behind Beren with their knives and grimaces drawn, but they couldn't get past Nyx's fire wall to engage the intruders.

"I've got this set," Beren told them, not bothering to turn around. "Go help the others finish things up—out by Dormitory Six, last I heard."

"Others?" the disarmed soldier repeated as the agents hurried off to the dormitory wing. "What others? If you had any combat forces on hand you would have made your move days ago. And I *know* you don't have another Gabriel Hound. You're bluffing."

"Probably just more weaklings like that floppy scarecrow who delivered your sword," his partner sneered. "They won't last thirty seconds against the rest of the company."

"Haven't you heard?" Beren smiled benevolently over the flames at his old comrades. "The battle's practically over. You and Haldor were the last two standing."

"*Liar.*"

"Of course you're right—there weren't any combat agents here earlier. The rest of your team is currently losing to a band of scientists, some robotic mops, and a highly motivated flock of dodos." He whistled to Nyx, and she expanded the flame wall to encircle the soldiers. "I would say you can ask your friends all about it from a detention cell. But I imagine they're going to imprison everyone separately, so there won't be much opportunity for swapping stories."

The woman snarled at him from inside the flaming ring.

"The last regiment of the Royal Guard won't be losing to a bunch of pathetic *nobodies*!"

"Too late," said Beren. He limped up the hallway toward the detention wing, Nyx's fiery corral forcing the soldiers to trudge along ahead of them. "Yet another lesson you failed to learn until it was too late, Malena: never underestimate the invisible."

CHAPTER 21
OF CANDLES AND CRANES

By the time Captain Solomon's crew joined Corvus and the scientists, the battle was nearly over anyway. Bronwyn had already returned from depositing her captive in a jail cell, and she and Corvus kept the soldiers so busy they were completely caught off guard when reinforcements arrived. The two groups prowled each other in a stalemate until Beren and Nyx joined the party, and Nyx used her ring-of-fire technique to round everybody up and march them over to the detention wing. When the soldiers in this hallway were securely locked away, she repeated the maneuver on the ones who'd gotten trapped in offices earlier. A few of the soldiers still had their weapons on them—disarming them during the transfer had seemed too risky—but Solomon wasn't worried; a couple of the scientists were already making plans for an adjustable resonance emitter that would find the proper frequency to turn any slipsteel in its vicinity into a pile of useless silver jelly. They'd have everyone disarmed long before they had time to entertain any bright ideas about escape attempts.

Erma did one last security sweep to make sure they hadn't missed anyone, then released the shields from all the doors (except the detention wing, of course.) Her voice came on the intercom system to relay the General's instructions; everyone was to gather in the dining hall to reunite family members who'd been separated.

Orion led the way to the dining hall, then parked himself on top of a table to wait with the clustered kids until their families came to claim them. The young agent's eyes kept roving around the room—on the lookout for the kids' families, or perhaps the rest of Solomon's team, Zed assumed—but he soon realized he was mistaken. When Corvus led the combined science and combat crew into the dining hall, Orion jumped off his perch and strode right past his lieutenant without a word. The sea of scientists parted to clear a path between Orion and Fatima, who seemed to have forgotten anyone else was in the room. It appeared Fatima was sticking with her conviction not to speak to Orion, but at the moment, they seemed to be getting along fine without any words at all.

Doctor Ubime and her apprentices moved methodically through the long tables offering to check out any injuries, but no one seemed to need any help. Most people were so busy hugging, or crying, or jabbering with friends to work off their nervous energy, that they couldn't do more than motion the doctor on with a wave or a shaken head.

After whispered conferences with Beren, Solomon, and Orion to make sure she had the entire story straight, the General called the group to order and filled everyone in on the details. Well, not *all* the details—Zed and Tuesday exchanged silent glances every time she left something out—but she assured the group that all the intruders had been captured and all base inhabitants had been accounted for, then commended everyone for following the emergency protocols and taking care of each other through the lockdown. She didn't mention anything about who the intruders were, or what they wanted, or how they managed to get in, but perhaps she wanted to keep that information with the leadership team. And of course the General couldn't report on the adventures of the group that escaped to the safehouse, because she hadn't been filled in on most of it yet. But for now, at least, they could breathe freely.

"Nice place you got here," said a voice over Tuesday's shoulder. She jolted back in surprise and saw a familiar scruffy face lingering behind her—Scrimbley had slipped into the crowd unnoticed. Her mother jumped up from her seat at the long cafeteria table and wrapped the smuggler in a delighted hug, like he was a dear friend she hadn't seen in ages instead of a scheming, money grubbing, vulture of a—

Nyx bulldozed past, and Tuesday's train of thought was derailed by Scrimbley's spluttering protests as the dog draped her front paws over the man's forearms and slurped his face with her massive pink tongue. It did not escape Tuesday's notice that her father was also shooting Scrimbley some rather dark looks.

"Still got yer, uh… *pet,* I see," Scrimbley remarked weakly. At last he managed to heave the dog off and wiped his face on his sleeve. "So, what's the plan?"

"The kids didn't mention you were involved in retaking the base!" Theadora gushed. "But of course—no one better for coming up with creative solutions."

Tuesday rolled her eyes. "We helped too, you know," she muttered.

"Of course you did, darling!" Her mother planted a kiss on the top of her head, then pulled Zed in for yet another hug. "And a marvelous job you did, too. I can't wait to hear all about it."

———

"So, what's the plan?" asked Scrimbley again. This time, he wasn't milling around a crowded dining hall, but propping his muddy boots up on the massive, polished table in the General's conference chambers. After the kitchen crew threw together a party buffet from the fruit and cheeses and other supplies they had on hand, the General had selected a team to quietly slip out of the celebration and join her in plotting the Resistance's next move. Tuesday was pleased that she and Zed had been invited, along with their parents, and Captain Solomon, and all the base department leaders. Nyx accompanied her person, as always. They'd even sent a messenger on hoversled to retrieve Obaachan from the Tilford Heath safe house. But she couldn't imagine any reason Scrimbley deserved to be there... unless they just wanted to keep an eye on him so he couldn't wander the base, pocketing unsupervised silverware.

Obaachan, Solomon, Penn, and Orpin had already traded brief explanations of the past three days with the leaders who got caught in the lockdown. Then Zed and Tuesday were grilled on every detail of their morning at Tyrren's palace. They'd never seen their father's face cloud darker than when Sylas's name came up, but no one else seemed to notice this—they were far more interested to learn that the leader of the Red Hand might pick and choose which information he passed on to his boss.

From the attack on the base, it was clear the Legion's loyalties (and priorities) were a mixed bag. If the Red Hand was just as unreliable, the Resistance might have an opening to pit Tyrren's henchmen against each other. Everyone agreed the time had come to confront Tyrren once and for all, especially before he realized a decent number of his soldiers were sitting in the base detention wing. But no one could agree on exactly how to do that.

"The Solstice festival is only two days away," Professor Orpin pointed out. "Tyrren will be making a public appearance at the capital city's parade. Why not do it then?"

"Do *what* then?" asked Penn. "Are we kidnapping him, or trying to take out the rest of the soldiers, or what?"

"No," said the General firmly. "Retaking Alexandria by force isn't the answer. He'll have every excuse to claim we're the villains. We must convince the people to reject him." She turned to her daughter in law, who was busy scratching Nyx's ears with a thoughtful frown. "Theadora—it's time."

All eyes fixed on Zed and Tuesday's mother, waiting. But she went right on frowning and stroking Nyx. The Gabriel Hound was tall enough that even sitting on the floor, her head drew level with all the people in chairs, and she returned their stares with her tongue lolling out.

After a lengthy silence, Theadora spoke. But though the entire council hung on her words, she seemed to be addressing Zed and Tuesday specifically.

"When we went into hiding in the other world," she began, "we had to choose different names in case any of Tyrren's spies came looking for us. Over there, most cultures pair a given name with a family name. But in Falinnheim, children are only given one name. When they reach adulthood, everyone chooses a title for themselves— something that describes them uniquely, to distinguish them from anyone else that may have the same first name. When I came of age and joined the Regent's Council, I knew it was especially important to choose a title that would reflect the qualities I hoped to contribute in my service to Falinnheim." She gazed into her children's eyes. "Do you know what title I chose?"

Tuesday and Zed stared back, shaking their heads in silence.

"I was known as Princess Theadora the Peaceful." She sighed heavily before going on. "Tyrren has betrayed Falinnheim. We cannot allow him to damage it any further. And I agree—the public return of a missing regent might be enough to convince people to take a stand. But Tyrren doesn't care what the people want—he'll just squash anyone who dares to speak against him. I refuse to accept that the only way to restore peace is to start a war. Far too many lives have been lost already."

Everyone turned in surprise as Obaachan piped up. "Who said anything about a war? We can pull the sheepskin off that old swamp monster without throwing a single punch, let alone killing anyone."

"So, what," asked Doctor Ubime, "we just stroll into Alexandria and politely ask Tyrren to get lost? The crowd will be swarming with disguised Red Hand agents, not to mention the rest of the Legion. We can't count on convincing *all* of them to stop following orders. How exactly are we supposed to pull this off?"

Obaachan didn't answer. She just reached into the pocket of her robe and pulled out an old toffee wrapper. Slowly, her bony fingers smoothed and creased and folded and unfolded, working the waxed paper with practiced ease until the crumpled red square took the form of an origami crane. "Do children still make these?" she asked conversationally. "All my friends liked to fold paper cranes when I was young. We used to write wishes on them and then hide them in tree branches or float them down creeks. There was a stall at the Kyoto market that sold beautiful squares of folding paper, in all different colors. But we rarely had any pocket change left for paper—we'd already spent all our spare minutes at the sweet shop. So we'd fold the candy wrappers instead. Children have a way of finding the beauty in forgotten things, don't you think?"

Penn opened his mouth—probably to ask what any of this had to do with defeating Tyrren, Tuesday assumed. (She was wondering that herself.) But the General silenced him with a glare, and Obaachan rambled on.

"My grandfather used to say that if you folded one thousand cranes, your wish would come true. A lot of the adults in the village thought that was silly. 'You can't change anything just by wishing for it,' they'd say. But every time I saw a candy wrapper crane peeking out from an elderberry bush, I remembered my own wish, and my daily troubles seemed a bit more manageable. There's nothing magic about the paper, of course, or the folding. But daring to hope helped me face my problems in a way magic solutions never could."

"I think I understand," said Captain Solomon. He turned to Theadora. "You don't have to whip people into a frenzy to fight on your behalf. But as a symbol of the way

Falinnheim used to be, you can help them remember their hope—hope for the way Falinnheim can be again."

Obaachan passed her crane down the table to Theadora. "Hope is the best kind of courage," she said with a wink. "And when people find their courage, they can do anything."

Zed glanced over at his mother. She was still avoiding the council's eyes, but now instead of petting Nyx she was turning the toffee wrapper crane over in her fingers.

"How can you be sure?" she said at last. "How can one tiny spark of hope possibly be enough?"

"You should come to tonight's Hanukkah celebration," Zed suggested. "The captain's got a story about oil and candles I think you're really going to like."

CHAPTER 22
TIME TO CLEAR
THE AIR

"Are you sure this is going to work?" asked Captain Solomon as Neri switched on the resonance ray.

"We already tested it on Beren's sword," the inventor assured him. "Worked like a charm."

Zed and Tuesday weren't allowed anywhere near the detention wing. At least, not since last Bounty, when they'd been arrested as spies themselves. But everyone on the General's council was eager to see the new invention in action, so when they gathered around the conference room table the next morning, the children were invited along to watch the proceedings on the wall monitor.

Solomon's entire crew assembled in the hallway outside the captured soldiers' jail cells, along with a physicist, an electrician, a mechanical engineer, and Supervisor Penn as safety monitor. Corvus and Bronwyn would be providing the muscle so Doctor Ubimbe could tend the prisoners' wounds and deliver their breakfast without getting attacked in the process. But the real reason they were attempting something as dangerous as opening up those cell doors was so Beren could have a long-overdue chat with his old colleagues.

The first cell belonged to a man Zed and Tuesday recognized instantly. The broken nose, those restless, darting eyes—this was the soldier who had held a sword to Zed's neck when his party ambushed them on the road to Kyoto.

He didn't even attempt to get up. The soldier leaned calmly back on the bench attached to the wall while Corvus and Bronwyn pinned his arms down. As the inventor had promised, the collection of cobbled-together parts in the hallway had melted the soldier's slipsteel weapon into nothing more than a silvery puddle, which had slithered out of its holster and onto the floor. Corvus gave the all-clear, and one of the scientists adjusted a dial on the side of the machine until the shiny goop solidified back into a cylinder. Corvus kicked it through the open cell door, where Penn snatched it up and stashed it in a large specimen tray. Then it was the doctor's turn to dab at a cut over the captive's eyebrow with disinfectant and leave some bread and fruit on the cell's side table.

When the doctor finished her rounds, Beren took her place in the crowded cell and addressed the prisoner. "It's been a long time, Titus. What's new? Other than taking a bunch of innocent civilians hostage, I mean."

The soldier's face broke out with a sinister grin. "Settle a bet for me, Beren. Finnegan insists your wife must be a witch, to be able to control that Gabriel Hound. But I've only seen it with those brats of yours, and it didn't seem to need any instructions. I think the beast must be hypnotizing *her*. We've wagered three hours on the answer. And I don't have three hours on me right now, so I'd really love to prove Finnegan wrong."

Tuesday's fists clenched so hard they started shaking. She scowled at the General's wall monitor. How *dare* that crusty old cockroach talk about her family like that! But apparently her father wasn't so easily baited, because he ignored the question altogether and tried to steer the conversation back to the attack on the base.

"Nice to see you're still making time for old friends. I'm really looking forward to chatting with Finnegan myself— he's locked up just down the hall, right next to Nicodemus, and Malena, and Haldor, and the rest of our old Royal Guard pals. What was the point of this little field trip, anyway? I heard you were looking for the Green Fly, but I can't imagine what the plan was after that."

"A traitor like you wouldn't understand, Beren. We stick together and help each other out instead of running off to hide."

"Like the time Sylas plotted with Tyrren to betray the regents, and your buddies decided to stick together and help him? He tried to kill me, you know. When I refused to go along with his plan, Sylas, personally, turned his sword on me. That's not what I'd call loyalty."

Titus just laughed. "That's what you get for not following orders. You started out as Sylas's apprentice, right? Disobeying your old trainer isn't what *I'd* call loyalty."

Beren let out a long-suffering sigh. "When we joined the Royal Guard, we took an oath. We promised to protect the regents at any cost. Somehow, it seems a lot of the guards cared more about protecting each other. I just don't understand how your sense of loyalty got so skewed… but I don't suppose I'll be able to change your mind about it now."

"We'll have to agree to disagree," said Titus, glaring. "I won't be taking morality lectures from a traitor."

It was no use arguing that point further. After a long pause, Beren circled back to his first question. "All right— let's say your gang's latest plan had worked. You discovered the Resistance base and captured their leader. Then what? How was any of this supposed to help you?"

Titus spoke like he was explaining simple arithmetic to someone impossibly stupid. "If we captured Falinnheim's most wanted fugitive, we could march him over to the palace and get our reward. We could finally show up those bigshot spies in the Red Hand. See, if we captured the Green Fly all by ourselves, Tyrren would have to admit he'd made a mistake in overlooking us for cushy palace jobs with his secret police. We're getting fed up with the constant travel for this rotating village patrol business."

"If Tyrren did you wrong, why go to all that trouble trying to win his attention now?" Beren argued. "Besides, I heard Tyrren doesn't choose Red Hand agents personally anyway. Didn't he put Sylas in charge of that? Say… come to think of it, how is it that our old lieutenant ended up with one of those cushy palace jobs, and the rest of you got sent away?"

Titus didn't answer. He suddenly looked a lot less smug.

"Was Sylas afraid you'd turn on him, next? Or maybe he didn't want the evidence of his scheme hanging around the capital, where people might put the clues together and start asking inconvenient questions."

Silence.

"We may have very different ideas about loyalty," Beren continued, "but there's one thing we can agree on: Sylas is the real traitor here. First, he talks half his guards into doing Tyrren's dirty work, then the moment the takeover is complete, suddenly the Liberator has no time for his most loyal supporters. Sylas becomes his right-hand man, and he conveniently forgets all about the friends that helped him get there."

Titus's frown had deepened into a full-blown scowl, now.

"Here's an idea—what if, instead of getting back at Sylas by licking Tyrren's boots, we give *both* those backstabbers what's coming to them?"

The soldier squinted skeptically at him. "You're going

after *Tyrren?* How?"

"You let us worry about that," said Beren airily. "The point is, for the moment, the Resistance and the last of the royal guard want the same thing. All you have to do is tell us about the security arrangements for Alexandria's Solstice festival. We'll take care of the rest."

The man's jaw unclenched. His face relaxed into its familiar calculating sneer. "What do you want to know?"

The team in the detention wing spent the rest of the morning making their way through the captured soldiers' cells. No one spilled the entire capital security plan, but each said enough that by the time Beren left the final cell, he was able to piece together where Tyrren would be and when. One soldier even let slip where they'd hidden their Legion uniforms when they changed into their miner's disguises. Sure enough, when Orion went to investigate, he found a pile of orange tunics and black scaled armor stashed in the janitor's closet of the busiest tavern in Kyoto.

While Orion was scouting in Kyoto, Corvus escorted everyone Fiona had gathered at the Tilford Heath safehouse back to the base. If this plan was going to work, they'd need all the help they could get.

When the night before the festival arrived, the plan was ready. As ready as it would ever be, anyway. All the Resistance leaders seemed confident, but Zed wondered if perhaps they needed to project a bit more confidence than they really felt. After all, there was no way to play it safe this time. If the plan succeeded, Falinnheim wouldn't need a resistance movement anymore. And if it failed… well, it's tough to resist much of anything from inside the palace dungeon.

It was barely past midnight when the wakeup call came over the intercom system. All over the base, the lights gradually blossomed from a faint glow to their full brightness, nudging everyone out of their blankets. A handful of volunteers would be staying behind to look after the poultry coop and detention wing, but the rest of the Resistance—more than four hundred people in all— had roles in the plan. It was six leagues to Alexandria; if they wanted to make it in time for the Solstice parade at noon, they were going to need an early start. And since Solomon's team had to be in place even earlier, they'd taken most of the available hoversleds. Everyone else had a long walk ahead of them.

After pulling on their cloaks and mittens and grabbing bundles of food for the road, Tuesday and Zed took their place in the crowd filing out through the hidden exit on the east side of the mountain. It wasn't as roomy as the export bay outside the crystal mine, or even the waterfall cave, but those were on the wrong side of the base to head for Alexandria. Waiting through a bottleneck at the door was still much faster than walking all the way around an entire mountain.

All the other kids from Professor Orpin's class would be walking with their families, but Tuesday and Zed had to make other arrangements. Since all the soldiers who recognized him were safely locked away, their father had finally been able to join Captain Solomon's team for a mission. Their mother would draw far too much attention in a crowd, so she had to be smuggled into the city in disguise. She and Obaachan had taken the last hoversled hours ago. That left Zed and Tuesday only one option; they would be making the journey supervised by the General herself.

They'd spent the past two days in meetings with the General's council, recounting every detail of their meeting with Tyrren and Sylas that might be useful. So they assumed today's journey would be business as usual— mostly just hanging out in their grandmother's orbit while she led meetings and gave orders. But as they switched on their crystal lanterns and tromped down the dark, snow-lined road, Tuesday realized the usual stream of department leaders reporting in with memos and waiting for instructions had completely dried up. Today, they were just three more faces in the crowd.

"I'm *not* the General," her grandmother replied, when Tuesday asked about the sudden lack of speeches and salutes. "Not today, anyway. We don't want to look like an organized protest—today we're all just normal villagers heading to the capital's celebration. We'll join other groups exactly like this the closer we get. People gather from all over Falinnheim for Alexandria's Solstice festival. This is my first undercover mission in years."

"We should have code names!" Zed suggested.

His grandmother raised a dubious eyebrow at him.

"So we don't accidentally give you away," he insisted. "We can't use our real names on an undercover mission. We've got to have a cover story."

A mischievous grin crept over Tuesday's face. "Great idea, Zed. From now on, I'm going to call you… Horatio Gornsblatt the Third."

Zed couldn't help it—he laughed. "No last names!" he protested. "Besides, if you get to pick my code name, then I'm picking yours. How about… Priscilla? Or Winifred?" But then he had an even better idea. He remembered a name he'd come across in a really old book about the American Revolution. "I've got it," he declared, returning his sister's wicked smile. "*Dorcas.*"

"Hey!" Tuesday yelped. She swung her lantern at him, but Zed dodged out of the way.

"Be nice to your sister, Horatio," the General scolded. But she followed it up with a wink.

"What about you?" Tuesday asked. "What's your name?"

"Well, that depends," the General replied slowly. "What's my cover story?"

Zed didn't miss a beat. "You're our grandmother, of course. Taking us to the Solstice parade."

"But that's *true,*" Tuesday reminded him, rolling her

eyes. "Not much of a secret identity."

"The best cover stories are as close to the truth as possible," the General declared. "Less chance you'll forget and mess up." She walked in silence for a moment while she considered.

"Call me Baba," she said at last. "That's what I called my grandmother."

Zed put on his most solemn face and offered her a handshake. "Nice to meet you, Baba. I'm Zed."

"You mean Horatio," Tuesday corrected him.

Zed smiled. "Not now, Dorcas. Baba and I have a lot of catching up to do."

CHAPTER 23
SHOWTIME

They arrived in Alexandria with two hours to spare. They'd passed the long hours of nighttime walking passing jokes and stories back and forth, occasionally stopping to rest their feet and sample the snack bundles the kitchen staff had prepared for everyone. By sunrise they reached the crossroads outside Persepolis, where the undercover Resistance group merged with the countless other caravans making their way to the capital city. By the time they reached the outskirts of the city there were so many revelers packing the streets that Tuesday had a lot of trouble picking any familiar faces out of the crowd. But that was exactly what they'd been counting on, Baba insisted. The Resistance needed to blend in, not stand out.

This left them plenty of time to act out their cover story of being regular kids, enjoying a festival with their grandmother. In the interest of making their act truly convincing, it was important to look like they were having as much fun as possible. So they sampled all the food vendors' stalls, pausing only to watch the magicians and jugglers and puppet shows dispersed through the streets surrounding Alexandria's main square. And they were so busy pretending to have a good time that once in a while, the impending mission slipped their minds, and they had a bit of genuine fun by accident.

Zed was strolling down Arcadia Street, happily munching fried pineapple poppers when he spotted it: just a flash of icy blue; two cold, calculating eyes spying on him through the crowd. His stomach dropped, his heart bolted for cover, and for one frantic instant he was convinced Tyrren somehow knew about the plan and was wading through the crowd to stop them. But then he remembered—Tyrren never got his hands dirty himself. And if the dictator showed up on a crowded street in person, he would have attracted attention long before now.

It was only a poster.

Tuesday caught up with him and frowned at the advertisement. "Looks like Eris has been hard at work," she grumbled. The illustrated Tyrren was looking as smug as ever, lounging lazily on a golden throne with one leg kicked up over the armrest. Like the posters Scrimbley had commissioned of their mother, this one also featured a symbolic crown hovering overhead. But it was positioned at a jaunty, tilting angle that somehow made Tyrren look careless, rather than regal. Bold letters at the bottom of the poster proclaimed: WOULD I LIE TO YOU?

Baba drifted up next to them and surveyed the poster. "This isn't one of ours…"

"Tyrren ordered his information minister to put up new ads," Zed explained. "Trying to make him seem trusted and powerful, and make Mom look like a criminal."

"Well, they're doing a terrible job," said Baba. "It's like the Green Fly debacle all over again."

Tuesday had a realization. "If I told you, 'Whatever you do, *don't* think about flying purple zebras', what's the first thing that would pop into your head?"

Zed laughed. "A flying purple zebra, of course. I wouldn't be able to help it."

"What's a zebra?" asked Baba.

"Never mind," said Tuesday. "The point is, the poster's message is backfiring. It doesn't make Tyrren seem trustworthy and respected at all. It puts his face right next to the idea of lying. And the crown really undermines his whole 'I freed us from the monarchy' scam."

They scouted the alley for more propaganda. And now that they'd noticed one, the others seemed to jump off the walls at them. There were murals and flyers everywhere, with headlines like THE LIBERATOR TAKES CARE OF BUSINESS and PROBLEM SOLVING FOR 16 YEARS AND COUNTING. But his sinister facial expression and intimidating pose made these seem more like threats than assurances. And the reference to "sixteen years" only reminded people Tyrren hadn't *always* been in power, and that the state of things before his reign hadn't been a problem for anyone but him.

They also found some of Scrimbley's posters of their mother. As Eris had promised, the headline had been changed to read WANTED: THE REBEL REGENT. A picture of a sword was scrawled over her right hand, and now an ominous cloud loomed behind her with gleaming fangs and electric blue eyes—symbolizing Nyx, they assumed.

"Is it just me," asked Tuesday, "or does this make Mom look… cool?" And she was right. Sure, a "wanted" headline typically meant someone was a fugitive from justice, but in this case, it almost read as if begging the princess to come back. The citizens of Falinnheim *wanted* her. And the illustration, too; the Rebel Regent character didn't come across as a villain—more like the main character of a fantasy video game. She couldn't look any more awesome if they'd thrown in sunglasses and a motorcycle.

"This new information minister has got to be the worst one he's had yet," Baba scoffed.

"No," said Zed with a growing smile. "In fact, I think Eris finally understands just how good she really is."

―――――

It was time.

The massive clock overlooking the city's main square announced the noon hour's arrival. The crowd condensed as everyone milling around the side streets pressed forward for a better view, and the people already occupying the square shuffled back to clear a path for the parade procession. Baba, Zed, and Tuesday wove through the wall of spectators until they neared the front, but not to get a better view of the parade. They had their own performance to prepare for.

A line of heralds blasted one long, ringing note from their silver trumpets to kick off the parade. They were followed by tumbling acrobats, then an army of jugglers, several firebreathers, a formation of marching drummers, and a parade float topped with a rotating model of the sun rising and setting over the palace. And last came the Liberator, gliding in on his lavish hoversled, surrounded by his entourage of diplomats and palace officials. The procession paused to allow Tyrren to descend from his floating throne, blow kisses to the crowd, and then climb the steps to the raised presenter's platform waiting behind him. Tuesday spotted Sylas lurking in the background of the platform with the rest of the palace diplomats, but as usual he melted into the scenery and let his boss take center stage.

"Showtime," said a voice in Tuesday's ear.

She flinched, but contained her surprise enough to avoid drawing attention. Scrimbley's scruffy face appeared next to Baba's.

Tuesday kept her eyes locked forward. "You're still here?" she hissed. "I thought you'd slink off long before now. Or are you holding out for another payday?"

Baba didn't look over either, but she shook her head slightly. "You might be surprised to know Scrimbley actually turned down my offer to pay him."

"What happened to looking out for Number One?" asked Tuesday.

"Funny thing," said Scrimbley. "I did some thinkin, and… well, I reckon maybe I don't have to do it all alone. Maybe what's good for everybody ends up working out square for me too."

"I knew Mom was right about you," Zed whispered proudly. "She saw who you really were all along. Even if you didn't."

Scrimbley allowed himself half a crooked grin. "Don't go tellin' nobody," he said with a wink. "Might spoil my reputation."

Tuesday scanned the packed square. She recognized a bunch of the Resistance members in the crowd, but they were spread out, pretending not to know each other. She also recognized a few of the uniformed soldiers stationed around the festival: Solomon, Corvus, Amira, Valis, Bronwyn, Orion… and her father, who edged his way through the sea of people until he stood at Baba's elbow. "Nice of my old colleagues to let us borrow these uniforms," he said quietly.

But of course the Legion had sent lots of soldiers to patrol the parade—real ones, who wouldn't be in on the plan. And there was no telling how many of the regular villagers would support them once the Resistance made its move. Or how many were not regular villagers at all, but Red Hand agents in disguise. Back in the base's council chambers, the plan they'd concocted felt bold. Daring. Ingenious, even! But now, with their last chance to call the whole thing off rapidly slipping away, Tuesday felt considerably less daring. More like she was stepping off a cliff with nothing but a homemade parachute.

"There are so many of them," Tuesday whispered. "Tyrren's followers run *everything*. They've got all the power. Are you sure this is going to work?"

"Not to fret," said Scrimbley. He pulled Neri's resonance ray out of his cloak and switched it on. "They may have the upper hand. But dealing underhanded always worked better for me anyway."

Tyrren took his place at the podium and raised his hands for silence. Hidden speakers carried his voice to every corner of the city as he began his speech, droning on about tradition and community and whatever else people expected in a Solstice address.

Zed whispered to Tuesday. "Ready, Dorcas?"

Tuesday took a deep breath, then nodded. "Okay, Horatio. Let's do this."

Together they ducked under elbows and around knees, picking their way through the last few people separating them from the front row of standing spectators. They emerged on the front line, stood, and waited. Normally, drawing the attention of a murderous dictator was the last thing they would have wanted. But this time, they were counting on it. They'd spent all week trying their best to be invisible; now, it was time to get noticed.

"…so on this shortest day of the year," Tyrren blathered, "let us take a moment to reflect—" He paused. His eyes swept the crowd, and when they landed on Tuesday and Zed he cocked his head to one side ever so slightly, like a dog that's trying to figure out whether someone actually threw a ball, or just pretended to. But then he smiled and picked up talking right where he'd left off. He made a subtle signal to Sylas standing behind him on the dignitaries' platform, who whispered to a somber-faced pair of men nearby, his eyes flicking over to Zed and Tuesday.

The men slunk off the back of the platform. Sylas went back to pretending to listen to Tyrren's speech.

Tyrren was just getting to the bit where he thanked all his loyal supporters when the agents reached their target. They stood behind the children, silent, so close Tuesday could feel hot breath against her neck. A hand clamped onto her shoulder.

Tuesday shrieked. She stomped backwards onto the man's foot, while Zed elbowed his agent in the stomach.

"Don't touch me!"

"I don't know you!"

"Baba, help!"

The plan unfolded like a line of falling dominoes, each

action triggering a fresh cascade of outrage. Tuesday slipped a mittened hand into her cloak pocket and pulled out the red gloves Corvus had confiscated from Kenry. She dropped them on the pavement as she darted into the clearing the parade had occupied earlier.

Baba pushed her way forward and thwacked one of the agents on the arm. "Don't touch my grandchildren!"

"The Red Hand!" shouted Scrimbley, pointing at the gloves.

"The Red Hand is abducting a child!" called Fatima. She clutched Fariq closer and lurched into Professor Orpin, who stumbled sideways and took out three more spectators standing nearby.

The audience traded concerned whispers. Officially, the Red Hand didn't exist. But everyone had heard the rumors...

Beren turned to Corvus, who locked eyes with Solomon, and so on through the square. In unison, the imposter soldiers pulled out their slipsteel batons. And since the Legion always sticks together, the real soldiers followed along. The resonance ray had all the swords locked in their inactive state, but the sight of weapons being pulled from holsters caused a collective gasp from the spectators.

Tyrren's voice came back over the speakers. "Please stay calm, everyone. Police business—nothing to worry about. They just located some missing children who got lost in the crowd. Stand back so they can take them to the administration tent to be reunited with their parents."

"Their grandmother is *right there*," Celia's father shouted.

"They're not lost. What do these 'police' want with them?" He pulled Celia closer, as though he feared Tyrren's agents might take off with her, too.

Beren limped forward and grabbed Zed by the shoulder. Corvus followed, snatching up Tuesday's arm.

"What are you doing?" yelled Penn. "Arrest the Red Hand, not the children!" The crowd murmured its agreement.

Tyrren tried to smooth things over. "No one's being arrested," he insisted. "Now if you'll all just—"

"Unhand my children." Theadora emerged from the shadows of the nearest alley. She strode forward, the ring on her forefinger glinting in the sun as she pulled off the hood concealing her face. Except for the ravens and floating crown, she was dressed exactly like the illustration on Scrimbley's posters, her pristine white robes billowing out behind her as she walked. Nyx followed, her eyes glowing but (for the moment) flames extinguished.

Tuesday caught a whisper over her shoulder, but it wasn't Scrimbley this time. She turned in horror to see another soldier standing behind her father.

When Solomon's team planned this mission, they were counting on the fact that no one would know they weren't really with the Legion. After all, every soldier who had served with Beren in the Royal Guard was currently locked in the base's detention wing. But they forgot someone. There was one more soldier who knew Beren's face—one who was far too young to be involved in the mutiny sixteen years ago: Leander, the soldier who had fought Beren and Nyx in the deserted Kyoto square last autumn. The one who had smashed Beren's foot trying to defend his patrol partner. The one who had, apparently, also been assigned to the Solstice festival's security team.

Leander's sword was harmless, trapped in its resting state like all the other slipsteel in the ray's vicinity. But the dagger he held against Beren's ribs wasn't.

"I take it you've captured Nicodemus," Leander whispered.

Slowly, Beren nodded.

"Is he alive?"

Beren nodded again.

"Good enough for me," said Leander. He didn't put the knife away, but his steely expression relaxed a bit. "Let's hear what the lady has to say."

CHAPTER 24
THE REBEL REGENT TAKES THE STAND

A fresh round of whispers rippled through the crowd as Theadora strode toward the podium. Normally, glimpsing a Gabriel Hound in the flesh would have set off a panic, but the way Nyx trotted calmly behind the woman they'd seen plastered all over Alexandria's walls and shopfronts had the audience transfixed. And if either of them looked dangerous, it wasn't the hound—the fire in Theadora's eye would have sent a dragon scurrying for cover.

"Enough." Even without a microphone, Theadora's voice rang through the square. "You have taken enough, Tyrren. For sixteen years, you have taken whatever you could get your hands on. You stole my home and my country. You stole the freedom and voices and *lives* of my people. You took my parents and grandparents, my brother and sisters and cousins. But you will not be taking my children."

"Nonsense," Tyrren scoffed. "Lies and slander. I'd expect nothing more from the Rebel Regent." He smirked, as though he expected this label to shame his opponent. But yet again, the spectators traded awestruck whispers. The Rebel Regent? At first they'd assumed this must be a prank, or some publicity stunt by an imposter. But if the Liberator himself confirmed she was genuine…

Theadora had nearly reached the speaking platform now. When she didn't back down, Tyrren motioned frantically to Sylas, but his intelligence chief didn't budge.

"Soldiers!" Tyrren called. "This woman is a wanted fugitive. Arrest her!"

Solomon's team, dressed in the Legion's distinctive orange tunics and black scaled vests, didn't budge either. And when the rest of the soldiers tried to shift their batons into weapons, they were stunned to find the slipsteel refused to obey.

Nyx glided in front of Theadora and up the steps to the platform. Tyrren tried to hold his composure, but he couldn't hold his ground—not against a beast that might maul him. Or burst into flames. Or both. Slowly, he backed into the far corner of the platform next to Sylas. The rest of Tyrren's entourage decided this was their cue to leave. They didn't even bother with the stairs—they jumped right off the back of the platform.

Theadora swept up the stairs and took Tyrren's place at the podium, while Nyx settled into a dignified pose at her side. The loudspeakers carried her voice across the city as she addressed the crowd.

"Sixteen years ago, the man you know as the Liberator was nothing more than a salesman, pestering the Regents Council with schemes he said would 'improve' Falinnheim. But the Moderator saw right through him—every plan he pitched was a thinly veiled attempt to secure money, power, and influence for himself at the people's expense. When he was finally barred from future dealings with the council, he concocted one more plot: this time, to have the Royal Guard overthrow the council and make him their ruler instead. And this time, he managed to convince enough followers to pull it off. Though many people bear responsibility for acting on this murderous scheme, Tyrren, alone, engineered it."

"Lies!" Tyrren snarled from his corner. "She plotted that all herself. She's blaming me for *her* schemes. Don't listen to this nonsense!"

Theadora pressed on. "As an eyewitness to the murders of the Regents Council, I was forced into hiding—not only to preserve my life, but to preserve the truth. I knew that surviving long enough to testify against him was the only way to bring Tyrren to justice."

"Imposter!" Tyrren interrupted. "She's just an actress. Can't you see? My enemies have dressed up a fraud to discredit me!"

"Which is it?" yelled a heckler in the crowd. It was

Dominic, who had Linus hoisted up on his shoulders for a better view. "First you say she's a regent who plotted the murders herself, and *then* you claim she's a fake? It can't be both!"

"Yeah!" Linus agreed. "That doesn't add up!" Their parents, standing nearby, nodded. There was a rumble of agreement from their neighbors.

"Look around," Theadora continued. "Who isn't here today? Every one of you knows someone who disappeared over the course of Tyrren's reign. Were any of them his supporters? No—without exception, the people who went missing are the ones who dared to speak against him. This is no coincidence. Tyrren will do whatever it takes to silence dissent—not because he is powerful, but because he is *weak*. He knows his selfish whims can't stand up to any kind of criticism, so he orders his secret police to make sure there is none."

"The secret police!" Tyrren spluttered, clinging to his last hope to deflect blame. "That's it—the Red Hand are behind all of this. They must be the ones who killed the regents! Soldiers, arrest—" He whirled around to point dramatically at Sylas, only to find the corner behind him empty. His eyes darted desperately through the crowd, but the agents he'd sent after Zed and Tuesday were long gone—they'd slunk away while everyone's attention was on Theadora.

"By killing anyone who speaks against him, Tyrren is just confirming what we already know—that words and ideas have power. He knows his selfish decrees are too flimsy to withstand the slightest breeze of dissent, that they can only stand when his is the only voice allowed to speak. Don't you see?" Theadora persisted. "Tyrren is *terrified* of you. He is terrified that we will finally learn: his greatest fear is also our greatest strength. He tells us that our voices are only a whisper, that it's pointless to bother arguing against him. But in his actions, he reveals the truth—our voices are what he fears most! Each voice alone might be a whisper. But combined, our voices can become a shout, a roar, a gale that will topple his murderous reign like a house of cards."

"We can work this out," called Tyrren. "The Red Hand have run off; they won't be able to oppress us any more. If you want more say in how things are run, maybe we can start a public comment forum on village bulletin boards, or—"

His voice withered. An ominous wave of noise was growing around the square—subtle, at first, but rising like the rumble of a gathering storm. Gentle rustling gave way to echoing calls, a haunting chorus of cronks and caws.

Ravens. On every tree branch and lamp post, rooftop and windowsill. Hundreds, maybe thousands of eerie black birds had descended on the city square. When the last of the flock settled into their perches the cawing died down, but it was immediately replaced by the awestruck whispers of the crowd below them.

"Are those crows?"

"No, ravens…"

"The royal bird—it's a sign!"

For the first time, Zed realized Fiona was missing. She usually perched on Corvus's shoulder, but that would have ruined his Legion disguise. He looked up at Corvus. "How did you get Fiona to…"

But Corvus just shook his head, staring at the feathered army gathering on every surface. "Wasn't me. Ravens don't usually make big flocks, remember?"

The loudspeakers broke through the confusion as the Rebel Regent resumed her address. "I am Princess Theadora the Peaceful, last regent of the old council. I have returned to claim my right as your leader—not to rule you, but to serve you. I cannot undo all the damage Tyrren's greed has caused, but I can serve as your Moderator, guiding and advising while you govern yourselves. Together, we can restore the peace and freedom Falinnheim once enjoyed."

"This is *treason*!" Tyrren bellowed. "Soldiers, to your duty! Silence her. Fight the entire mob if you have to. Anyone who opposes the Liberator is a traitor to Falinnheim!"

The spectators jeered at being called a mob, which got the ravens started scolding again. Across the square, all the soldiers looked around for their commanding officers. Their conflicted glances all carried the same message: did he just order them to attack unarmed civilians?

Beren whispered to his captor. "What do you think, officer?"

Leander was silent for a moment. "I took an oath," he

said at last. "But not to the Legion—an oath to the law. To do what's best for Falinnheim. And if she really is the last regent, the law is on her side." He lowered his knife, then slipped it back into a hidden sheath in the top of his boot.

Beren gestured to Scrimbley. Scrimbley switched off the resonance ray. Leander pulled out his slipsteel baton, which dissolved in his hands and reemerged as a pair of heavy shackles connected by a chain.

Tyrren's jaw dropped as the crowd parted, allowing the young man to approach the podium. "Mutiny," he squeaked, "that's what this is! Somebody stop this lunatic—"

Two more soldiers waded through the audience to join Leander. They marched up the steps, swords held at the ready, and passed behind Theadora and Nyx to the edge of the platform. Tyrren just stood there, wringing his hands. Every moment, he looked more and more like a cornered animal.

"Tyrren the Liberator," Leander announced. "You have been credibly accused of murder and conspiracy. By the authority of the Legion, I am placing you under arrest to await trial."

Tyrren threw his hands up to shield his face, as though he feared the two soldiers brandishing swords might attack him. Leander pressed the shackles into the cringing dictator's exposed wrists and allowed them to harden in place. An extra length of chain sprouted out of one end, which Leander used to lead Tyrren down the steps and off the platform.

"Wow," Zed commented. "I never thought we'd be on the same side of *anything* as the Legion."

But Tuesday didn't answer. She couldn't hear him over all the cheering.

———

It was snowing again.

A week had gone by since the Solstice festival, which Zed and Tuesday spent back at the Resistance base. The first few days were a blur of endless festivities—celebrating the Solstice, and the last days of Hanukkah, and then Christmas. But mostly, everyone credited the jubilant mood to the fact that over in Alexandria, Tyrren was sitting in the palace's dungeon instead of its throne room.

Now that everyone was all partied out, things were starting to get back to normal. Well, almost normal. Zed and Tuesday had returned to their morning ritual of eating breakfast with Dad in the base security office. Mom and Baba were busy with endless meetings, as usual. School had started back up, and of course there were still chores to be done. But underneath all the mundane routines and responsibilities surged a current of anticipation. No one at the base seemed willing to bring it up, but everyone understood: with nothing left to resist, life for the Resistance was about to change.

"Better get moving," said their father, who was busy scanning the frigid landscape through the security monitor. "It'd be a shame to be late on your last day of school."

It wasn't Tuesday and Zed's last school day ever, of course—just their last day at *this* school. Tomorrow, their family would be moving to Alexandria. The Rebel Regent had a lot of work to do.

When they arrived at the classroom, they found the usual pre-class chaos: a symphony of dueling conversations, and squabbles over the best seats, and kids digging around for their missing books and pencils and science projects. But one thing was different: today, instead of Professor Orpin trying to get everyone organized and quiet, someone else stood at the front of the room.

"Obaachan?" said Tuesday in surprise as Zed closed the door behind them. "What are you doing here?"

"Substitute teaching, of course. What does it look like I'm doing, the Tango?" She winked at them. "The professor took the day off. I heard he's doing some martial arts training with Lieutenant Corvus today."

"But Solomon's agents are disbanding," Zed pointed out. "Isn't it a bit late to try out for the Operations team?"

"That's why it's perfect timing," Obaachan argued. "Corvus has plenty of time on his hands to teach him. And with so many people moving out of the base, it might be Orpin's last chance to learn from an expert. He may not get to use these skills at work, but everyone needs a hobby— might build up his confidence a bit. Besides," she finished with another wink, "the exercise will be good for him."

Tuesday and Zed plopped down on a sofa at the back

of the room and waited for the babble to die down. Fariq was already there, trying to squeeze in a few more pages of reading before class got underway.

"It's my last day too," he said, without looking up. They hadn't discussed their family's moving plans in class, but as usual Fariq seemed to absorb information from his surroundings, picking up the clues people didn't even realize they left behind.

"Where is your family heading?" Zed asked. "Back to your hometown?"

Fariq shrugged. "We don't really have a hometown. My parents met at the base, so I've never lived anywhere else. But Auntie Fatima wants to move to West Thebes, and Grandad is coming with her. So we all decided to go."

"What made her choose West Thebes?" asked Tuesday. "Is that where she grew up?"

Fariq shook his head, but kept on reading. "No. But Orion did. He went there a couple days ago to visit his mom, and he brought Auntie with him. Auntie says she liked the village so much she wants to live there. But what she really means is Orion plans to live there, and she wants to be near her boyfriend. She doesn't call him that, but I know." He closed his book and looked up. "I'm sure the village is nice, but it doesn't really matter where we live," he concluded. "As long as our family sticks together, things will work out okay."

"I wish we could do that," Zed sighed. His mother

was needed to straighten things out in the capital, and of course he and Tuesday and their father were coming with her. Nyx, naturally, tagged along wherever Mom was. But Baba wouldn't be joining them in Alexandria—not yet, anyway. The Resistance might be breaking up, but many of its members had only ended up at the base because they had no other homes to go to. All those people needed a safe place to stay until they could locate new jobs and housing. And without ties to a specific village, they had all of Falinnheim to choose from, so getting everyone resettled was going to take some time. Luckily, the General had lots of experience getting people organized.

"Stop moping," said a haughty voice behind them. Celia came around the back of the sofa and perched herself on the arm. "You're going to live in a palace, with cooks and servants and bodyguards and everything. What have you got to complain about?"

Tuesday frowned at her. "You know none of that was my idea. I'd rather be going *home*."

The girls regarded each other in silence for a moment. But then Celia smiled. "I have to admit, your mom did a pretty good job with her speech and all. And that trick with the ravens—no idea how she pulled that off, but it had style. I suppose if someone has to live in luxury, better her than Tyrren." She clapped Tuesday on the back, then wandered off to find a more comfortable seat. "Maybe once you get the place fixed up you can take me on a tour.

I've always wanted to see the palace from the inside."

Tuesday chuckled. "Sure thing, Celia. A class reunion would be fun. We'll make it a field trip."

Obaachan thumped the floor with her walking stick to call the class to order. Everyone got quiet and faced the front of the room, and Zed brightened a bit. At least Obaachan was coming with them to Alexandria, he remembered. Maybe she could convince Baba to visit once in a while for Grandma Boot Camp.

"I have no idea what's coming next," he whispered to Tuesday, "but whatever happens, at least we'll tackle it together."

His sister shushed him. "Quiet, Horatio. Can't you see the lady's trying to teach?"

Zed laughed and shook his head. "Whatever you say, Dorcas."

www.ingramcontent.com/pod-product-compliance
Lightning Source LLC
Chambersburg PA
CBHW050838190726
48286CB00007B/2142